THE

PHYSICS

of

THIΠGS

GIΠΠY FITE

MILFORD
HOUSE
an imprint of Sunbury Press, Inc.
Mechanicsburg, PA USA

MILFORD
HOUSE

an imprint of Sunbury Press, Inc.
Mechanicsburg, PA USA

For information about special discounts for bulk purchases, please contact Sunbury Press Orders Dept. at (855) 338-8359 or orders@sunburypress.com.

To request one of our authors for speaking engagements or book signings, please contact Sunbury Press Publicity Dept. at publicity@sunburypress.com.

FIRST MILFORD HOUSE PRESS EDITION: October 2022

Set in Adobe Garamond Pro | Interior design by Crystal Devine | Cover by Ginny Fite | Edited by Abigail Henson.

Publisher's Cataloging-in-Publication Data
Names: Fite, Ginny, author.
Title: The physics of things / Ginny Fite.
Description: First trade paperback edition. | Mechanicsburg, PA : Milford House Press, 2022.
Summary: A dying woman explores her memories and discovers who she is and how she survived her complicated childhood. *The Physics of Things* is about the triumph of love and the resilience of the human spirit.
Identifiers: ISBN : 979-8-88819-006-7 (softcover).
Subjects: FICTION / Women | FICTION / Short Stories (single author) | FICTION / Literary | FICTION / Coming of Age.

Product of the United States of America
0 1 1 2 3 5 8 13 21 34 55

Continue the Enlightenment!

❦

To my sons Hal, Peter, Josh, Mike, and Matt,
who taught me everything important.

And to Lori.

Also by GINNY FITE

Cromwell's Folly

No Good Deed Left Undone

Lying, Cheating, and Occasionally Murder

No End of Bad

Blue Girl on a Night Dream Sea

Possession

Co-author of Thoughts & Prayers

I Should Be Dead by Now

"We tell ourselves stories in order to live."
—Joan Didion

CONTENTS

AT LAST, BLISS

I sit in the garden, surrounded by white daisies with yellow centers, spears of blue Russian sage, and lavender-colored lilac blooms. A pinwheel of smells swirls around my face, changing colors. I'm unsure how I got here. My hands and the dirt blend—earth spreads up my arms, smelling green. Green light, chiming like bells, weaves its way toward me. My head is a balloon untethered to my body. Floating is beautiful. I am free.

The light amazes me, enveloping me in wave after wave of color. I hear a sound. My mouth, tongue, and lips frame delight in a way that seems to come from someone else. I lie back on the ground, and my body zooms toward blue, an infinite blue hovering above me, a sky of dreams.

I don't know how long I lie there this way. Then my brain says *something is wrong*. I wait a while to see if it will say something else. I have a crushing headache. *You have to do something, we're in trouble*, my brain warns as if it operates separately from me and knows better, as if there are two of us in here, as I always suspected. I want to say, *Hello, it's about time we met*, but I don't have any words.

I gather myself and find I'm on my knees. I pat my pockets, looking for something I immediately forget. The world is so beautiful; everything is so beautiful that I lose track of what I'm doing. Blue mountains shimmer in the distance. My entire body yearns for them. I want to absorb them, to pull them under my skin and feel their bulges reaching up into that blue sky. I sit down on my feet.

Call for help, my brain instructs. I look down at the screen of the phone in my hand. It's blank. I can't remember how it works. I try talking to it. I can't remember numbers or names. "Call . . . ," I sound like a crow. I look around for the bird that made that sound

1

and accidentally touch the screen with my thumb. It awakens and says something to me, but I can't understand it. I weep.

Ask for help, my brain urges. I hear my voice saying, "Ah, ah, ah, ah. . . ."

My left arm goes limp; I fall endlessly, and my spirit lifts and surrenders. I separate from my body. This is bliss.

I hear people talking around me, moving me. I feel their urgency, their compassion. We're all moving. A horrible blaring sound encases me. I float above them and look down at my body.

"We're losing her," a man says.

I want to comfort him, but I have no words and can't move my hand.

By the light drifting into the room, it's early morning. I wake thinking of my children in sets—sons and daughters-in-law and their children—believing they're safe even though I can't check on them. I was dreaming about my husband and stepmother coming back from the dead in a Jeep. Sometimes they ride together, sometimes alone. A cat slept on the engine of the vehicle after it stopped.

They seemed to be friends, and she was telling me something about him. I was supposed to pick him up, or I was not. Sometime before this, I had taken a pair of shoes, a pendant, and something else I wanted on my way to meet him. I was eager, young, and in love.

The entire neighborhood was an open-air market with goods displayed in booths with vibrantly colored awnings. Palm trees swayed above us. A woman whispered over my shoulder that it was okay to take what I wanted. Soft silk persimmon saris, piles of jade and tourmaline bracelets, necklaces of rubies and garnets, pyramids of oranges, stacks of books. Such unexpected riches.

I imagine a hospital room, the corner of a sheet folded down, light from the window forming a parallelogram of light on the floor. And then wakefulness to beeping and shouts on the hospital PA system, the nurse badgering me with questions. "Can you tell me your name?"

Someone is crying inconsolably in the hallway, and I hear the ache of it dancing with whispered consolation. Someone presses my hand, and I press back. I recognize my son's face, and a thousand delights cascade through me—he's born, he throws his small arms around my neck, kisses my cheek, smiles at me from across a large room, and runs toward me, saying, "I love you, Mama,"—our hearts are connected by a thousand different colored filaments all glowing now. A word finds me. *Blessings. Yes, blessings.* And gratitude, as rich as the dirt I sink my fingers into, as deep as the heart of the earth.

I close my eyes and find myself hanging upside down on the metal jungle gym in the next quad over, swaying above the asphalt ground below me. The world tilts, and I can understand how the universe is saddle-shaped and infinite. My sister says, "Daddy is going to die, and I don't want to be there when he does." A translucent blue-green wave lifts me off my feet, and I float on my back, facing the sky. Cool water embraces me and caresses my limbs.

Now I'm holding onto a thick rope bigger than the grip of my hand. Waves are coming toward me. My mother yells, "Hang on!" Then she laughs the laugh that scares me. The wave moves over my head. I keep my eyes and mouth closed. When it passes, I can breathe for a second, and then another wave, clear green and taller than the first, is on me, high above my head. I hold fast to the rope, and when the wave passes, I try to gulp air before the next one comes. I hear my mother's laughter, louder and giddy, uncontrolled. Strong hands grasp my body. A man scoops me up and carries me to the beach. I hear him say, "What's the matter with you?" to someone behind him. "Didn't you see she was drowning?"

I open my eyes to my grandchildren surrounding my bed. They're so beautiful, wearing their serious faces. I long to hold them all in my arms at once, to hear them giggling. I spread my arms, and they engulf me. I close my eyes. It's okay now. I can go.

I find a quarter lying in the snow on the top step leading to the back of the large Tudor house on the Jesuit college campus where I work. It's just enough for my morning coffee donation. The old priest, who meticulously keeps the alumni donation records on two-by-four index cards, updating them by hand, has a desk in the back of the building near the coffee station. He is, like me, the least of us. I say good morning to him every day.

He never turns on the overhead fluorescent light, using instead the old brass lamp that sits on the corner of his huge mahogany work surface. Light illuminates his corded hands. I go up to his desk, show him the quarter in the palm of my hand, and say, "See, Father, God loves me."

He looks up at my face, beaming. "I always knew that."

In the chapel, the sound of voices in close harmony fills the space to the brim until it waterfalls down the walls and leaps up as waves of joy. The sweet thread of a single soprano voice solos and light streams through stained glass windows like music, and I understand the word exalted.

Time is irrelevant. Every so often, a dear face comes close to me, and lips brush my cheek. If I could speak, I would tell them not to be afraid, but I'm tired, so tired, and I drift away.

Going sixty-five miles an hour, my car hits rubber poles stuck in the asphalt where my lane used to be. The car veers into the left lane. The steering wheel doesn't respond to my grip. I jam my feet on the brake and clutch and watch the car float across the left lane into the metal guardrail. The front of the car collapses slowly, the guardrail coming toward me, accompanied by the screeching sound of metal against metal. My head hits the steering wheel, then the top of the partly opened window.

I open my eyes and see the steering wheel. I turn my head to the right. Searing pain shoots through my brain; my leg and hip scream. I close my eyes. Something wet trickles down my face. I touch my forehead and look at my hand. *Blood*, I tell myself, as if it's someone else's. I close my eyes again. Someone talks to me. I see a police officer sitting in the passenger seat. He says the ambulance is on the way.

"You have to call my kids," I mumble. He asks for the number. I can't remember my number or any numbers. I clamp down on panic and tell him my address book is in my purse. He pulls it out and asks for a name. I can't remember any names. "You have to get to my kids," I beg him, then close my eyes.

4

The EMTs talk to me, saying what they're going to do. They lift my gray sweater and put white pads on my chest. They put an IV in my arm. I'm glad I have on clean underwear. My grandmother would be pleased. I hear her telling me, "Always wear clean underwear in case something happens to you."

As they load me into the ambulance, pain slices through me and then fear. I might die from this. My breath comes in quick spurts. The EMT sitting with me puts a hand on my shoulder and tells me, "Don't worry, just breathe slowly. Take deep, slow breaths." I practice what he says.

I'm floating above my body, looking down at the ambulance from the ceiling. I'm peaceful with no worries, not even tired anymore. The scream of the siren is a thousand miles away, clearing a path for someone else.

When I open my eyes, the doctor explains I've had a stroke. As he talks, long black lines squiggle out of his mouth, slither across the walls, and out of the door. I hear the black lines swishing through the halls, going somewhere else where someone will understand them.

My son tells me I'm going to be all right. The doctors are doing everything they can.

I smile at him. "I am. I know. I'm all right," I try to say. I want to lift him into my arms the way I used to and feel his head on my shoulder, his soft curls brushing my cheek, feel the breath move his chest in and out against me—*my beautiful boy*.

I'm wearing my favorite purple jumper, and I'm lost. I'm trying to find my grandmother's apartment. None of the buildings around me are familiar. I've gone too far, missed my turn. The wide street stretches out to my left, with cars, buses, and trucks whizzing by. Soot blows up from the street in a cloud and drifts toward me. Fear overpowers me. I put my hand over my mouth to keep myself from crying. I'm sure I've been walking for hours.

And then I see a street I recognize and turn into it. It takes me past houses I vaguely remember and then right up to my school. I wasn't far away after all; just confused. I turn right at the alley, go through the showers, make another right at the clotheslines, and walk to my grandmother's building. I open her door, walk into the living room, and crawl into her lap. She's watching *Queen for a Day.*

"*Mein Kind,*" my grandmother says, hugging me against her huge, soft bosom, rocking slightly in her chair. "*Shayna punim,* where have you been?"

"I was lost, Grandma, lost all over the projects, but now I've found you."

"*Ach,*" my grandmother says, "I have been lost also. It is a terrible feeling. I am so glad you found me." She holds me tightly and kisses the top of my head while the woman on the television show jumps up and down because she has won a new washing machine.

Now I see it's snowing pink petals. I hold my infant to my breast and, in the next instant, nestle my hand in my father's and look up at him. I drip water from a straw into my mother's mouth. My sister, sitting in the morning sunlight with her hands in her lap, is beautiful. I weep as each son leaves me for his future. I stand in the stirrups and gallop on a horse across a field, screaming with delight and fear. I hold my new grandson in my arms, and the whole universe moves into me, and God is real and understandable, no longer a mystery. I watch undertakers zip my husband into a body bag.

I see the entire canvas, every color, every shape, and pattern, glowing and moving, forming, and reforming. And then I see the white between the points of color and the radiant shapes of things I didn't see before, couldn't know, and how the brilliant surface reflects only light, all light, all being, and nothing at all.

I am everything—all sound, color, dark, soft, sharp, and falling free. I know nothing. I know everything. Light holds me. I wrench myself from bliss, blow a kiss, and wave goodbye to my grandson.

He waves back to me and says, "Bye-bye, baby."

VALLEY OF THE SHADOW

My first-grade teacher snaps her fingers, her arm extended in my direction to make me look at her and gives me her "behave" look. I duck my head and stare at my hands.

It's quiet in the classroom except for the sound of wooden sticks hitting the inside of paste jars, the rustle of dying leaves, and breath. We're pasting leaves onto a piece of paper. I don't tell anyone, but I secretly believe the shapes of leaves match the outline of the grown trees they fall from—the way calves look like cows—when a different question leaps into my mind, presses itself into my mouth, and I forget to raise my hand.

"Does it hurt the leaves when they change colors?"

I think about my skin turning yellow, then orange, red, then brown, dying of thirst, turning itself inside out, falling away from me, curling up at the edges, swept to the curb by a breeze.

"Focus, Irene," the teacher says, her skin stitched together above her mouth by tiny black hairs. She taps the desk and turns her face away from me but says in a muffled voice, "No, I don't think so."

My skin hurts from imagining the death of the leaf in my hand. For a second, I'm deaf and miss an instruction. Then I hurry to catch up, fumbling with the glue. White paste sticks to my fingertips, and later when it's dry, I peel it off and watch it float to the floor.

I want to be outside running through the turning leaves, inhaling their burnt umber smell. Instead, I'm trapped with all the other children inside this new three-story elementary school with 1950 carved into the corner of the brick building. I'm the opposite of free, learning about standing in lines and responding to bells, about sitting at

7

a desk with my hands folded. Silent. Another child's eyes wander to the window and rest. Sky reflects in them. We're all longing for the same thing, but we're supposed to raise our hands to ask a question, speak only when called on, and pay attention. Those are the rules, and I must learn them.

I'm desperate to be good at school. My life depends on it. Every school morning, my heart curls into a tight ball in my chest, hoping for shelter. I pray I won't make any mistakes, won't speak out of turn, and that I won't do the wrong thing, but praying is not enough to curb my tongue, as the teacher insists. I imagine my tongue parked near the sidewalk as close as it can get, lapping the lemon ice cement.

My teacher and the principal stand in the classroom doorway, talking in low voices. "She's incorrigible," the teacher says and points at me. Then she throws back her head, so her chin points at the ceiling and laughs. The principal covers her mouth with her hand. I have no idea what incorrigible means, but from her laugh, I guess it isn't so bad unless she's laughing at me. A clenched ball rises bitter in my throat, making my mouth sour.

"Heads down. Thumbs up," the teacher calls out, looking at me.

I turn my head and peek as thirty children, whose feet swing beneath their seats, put their heads down on desktops on command and hold their thumbs up in the air. We're learning to obey; the teacher tells us this every day. I have no idea why obedience is important or when I will need it, but the teacher rewards those who mind her.

We all want gold stars for good behavior. Each day, the teacher prints the names of the class stars on the blackboard. I want to be on that list; I want to be acknowledged for my effort. Gold stars are as important as cleanliness, something the teacher tells us is next to godliness. I have no idea what godliness is, but it must be important because the teacher says it is.

I crave stars more than cookies. Demerits, a word so heavy in the teacher's mouth that her lips turn down when she says it, must be avoided.

"What's a demerit?" Even though asking questions without raising my hand is bad, I can't stop my mouth from speaking the words.

The teacher's black eyebrows meet over her nose. Her lips form a thin line above her sharp chin. She makes a mark in her book with her pen. "A demerit is the black mark right next to your name in my book." She holds up her marking book for all of us to see.

My eyes widen. The air in my nose is cold. I hold my breath, and my heart stops for one beat, two. I have failed again. I want to disappear into the air and leave no trace.

Every morning, we pledge allegiance to the flag, our hands on our hearts. We say the "Lord's Prayer" in unison. Billy fumbles with the word "temptation," saying it a second later than everyone else. I giggle. The teacher glares at me. I wonder if temptation is the place children go when they're bad.

My mother says we're Jewish, and I don't have to say these prayers, but I do because not saying them would give me demerits. She says I go to a public school, and they can't force religion down my throat. Even at six years old, I understand the dangers of resistance. The teacher will talk about me to the principal or send me to the office. Other children will stare at me, point, and giggle. No one will sit with me in the lunchroom. I want to be the same as everyone, not different. I want to be safe.

The teacher reads "Psalm 23" to us. She holds the Bible open across both her hands as if it's a delicate flower she just picked from her garden. The pages are as thin as skin. She reads to us about the valley of the shadow of death and the presence of enemies. I lose myself in the valley long before we get to goodness and mercy. I wonder if God made school rules, and that's why they're so important.

These rules don't bind my world outside school. In my home world, other laws matter. Being alert is rewarded. Noticing small things that could become bad news—my mother suddenly turning away from the stove with that wild look in her eye, a fork in the wrong place, steam rising from the bath—could save me. Running fast, hiding well, and being as quiet as dust falling all get me invisible gold stars.

In my real world, the rules change every day. I've learned how to make a new plan on the fly. I have maps in my head of various ways to go home and two different routes that lead to my grandmother's apartment in case bad people block my path. Bad people are everywhere, my mother says, ready to spirit me away at a moment's notice. She knows the bad people are coming; she can see things before they happen. She can see what I'm thinking. I deliberately memorize landmarks for navigation. I'm constantly on alert; my real world is not about godliness.

But even in school, rules loosen when we go outside for recess. We're allowed to use our outside voices. We run in circles, screeching like gulls at the beach. Sometimes I just stand there and watch the other kids. Sometimes I make a beeline for the swings.

One day, mid-way across the playground, I see my father, and I stop moving. He doesn't belong in my school world, standing in the playground, and waving at me. He calls me and beckons. "Hey, Mouse. Come here." He smiles.

I remember him coming to another school. I was younger, and my memory comes in gusts of images blowing through me. A high chain-link fence surrounded us. Children bundled in winter clothes climbed through barrels. I was small enough to stand up inside the barrel. My sister, Sarah, was in a crib inside the building. My father stood on the sidewalk on the other side of the fence.

I ran to him. He put his fingers through the link and wiggled them. I wrapped my hand around his two fingers. He said something, and for a minute, I was warm, the kind of warmth that traveled up my arm to my chest and face and made me smile.

A teacher put her hands on my shoulders, said something sharp to him, and led me away. I looked back but didn't say anything. He waved. I longed to put my nose against his for an Eskimo kiss.

Now I'm in first grade and supposed to know better. He calls my name again. He wears his plaid wool jacket, the itchy one that smells like snow got caught in it. Sun glints off the flat top of his crew cut and the end of his nose. His smile pulls on my heart. He reels me in. I run to him without thinking, knowing I'm breaking another rule I don't understand, but that doesn't matter. Everything I want is where he is.

I know I'm not supposed to see him during school time. I look around. None of the other children's parents are here. But I must run to him; all the impulses in my body require it. There's no thought in this. A million demerits don't matter. The hair on my arms stands up and leans in his direction. I can't help myself. I can already smell his cigarettes and cough drops, already feel myself in the safety of his arms. He'll call me Mouse and nuzzle the top of my head with his chin. He is my safe world, the place where I would rather be.

He takes my hand, and we walk over to a bench clear at the other end of the schoolyard, far from my classmates and the first-grade entrance to the building. He has his lunch with him in a brown paper bag. He gives me a cherry cough drop and starts peeling the orange he takes out of the bag. He's talking in that low rumble I like. I don't listen to the words; it's the sound I crave. It's better than a hundred million gold stars, better than godliness.

I eat an orange segment he hands me. Cherry and orange explode together in my mouth. I look around to see if the teacher is watching. By my count, I've now done at least two wrong things. I wonder if this quaking in my chest is how the valley of the shadow of death feels.

Without warning, the school bell clangs. The sound bounces off every bone in my body and bangs in my skull. My pulse leaps: recess is over. I jump up and run as fast as I can toward the building. I can't be late, shamed by the teacher for tardiness. I can't bear standing in the corner, my cheeks burning. Everything important in my world is sitting on the bench, and I'm running away from it.

My father runs after me, calling my name over and over. The distance between his voice and me becomes longer. I want to return to him, but I must go into the building. The bell is ringing. I must be in my classroom, in my seat, before it stops. The rule is certain; there's no room for special circumstances. I've learned this the hard way. My heart twists, but I run away from him. My feet pound across the asphalt.

At the double doors where my teacher watches over us, I turn around and see my father has stopped ten feet away from me. He gently turns a child who blindly runs into him while trying to get to the door in time. Strangled by tears I can't allow to escape, I step into the building and my stomach knots.

My father calls out, "Goodbye, Mouse. Goodbye." He waves.

He doesn't come for a visit with me that night, or the next night, or the one after that. I wait for him to open the door, scoop me up into his arms, and ask me about my day. On the fourth night, he calls. My mother hands me the phone. "It's for you."

It's my first phone call. From now on, all phone calls in my life begin with a small twinge of dread.

I hold the black receiver in both hands and listen to the sound of his voice. He asks about my day at school. I tell him we have a baby duck in a cage and that the cage smells funny. He sings a lullaby, and I pay attention to every word. He says we're going to count to three together, and then we'll hang up at the same time, so neither of us is left waiting for the other to say something more.

Taught to follow instructions, I hang up the phone on three, but I'm still that word the teacher called me—incorrigible. I stay by the phone, watching it, thinking it might ring again and my father will say he's coming right now. He's changed his mind. He'll be here in a minute. I wait for my next breath, the next word, the next ring. My heart slows. I am waiting for more instructions.

"He'll see you next Saturday," my mother says, flipping through her magazine.

I walk to my bedroom, feeling as if everything inside me—muscles, bones, and blood—have vanished. Only my fragile outer shell moves through space. I must be careful not to make any sharp moves, or my skin will drift away, change colors, and drop to the floor, and I will disappear completely.

I count the days until next Saturday on my fingers. I stare at my hands. His absence is my punishment for sitting with him on the bench in the school playground. I've broken the rules, and they've taken away the shepherd who guides me.

"Go to bed now," my mother calls from the kitchen.

I lie down.

GOING TO THE DOGS

From the top of a hill behind our apartment building, standing next to the new chain-link fence that separates our projects from Dayton Street, I watch my friend, Butch, talk to two big kids at the bottom of the hill where the grass meets the cement sidewalk. They tower over him. My fingers curl around a metal link in the fence while they talk.

We'd snagged cardboard squares from the cellar, and Butch taught me how to sled down dead grass. All the other kids have gone in. The sun is going down. It's winter, cold, but no snow. A chill sneaks under my jacket, stealing the warmth from my body, but I don't want to stop. I'm getting good at this game.

I bite the fingertip end of my blue mitten with the white snow-flakes on it, pull my hand out, and stuff the mitten in my pocket to get a better grip on the board. I tug my knit hat back over my ears and watch the kids. From where I'm standing, I can see my kitchen window at the back of my apartment building.

Butch lives one building over from me. We've grown up together, we're in the same class, and I think of him as a friend, someone to play with but not a person in whom I confide. At eight years old, I know there are different kinds of friends. I'm still deciding about him. Even with real friends, I'm learning there are always secrets you keep. We are, each of us, a hive of secrets; I hear the buzzing even when we don't speak.

※

My mother, sister, and I live in the good projects, the safe ones where there's no crime, the garden kind built with bricks and only three stories high, surrounded by trees and grass. The difference between good and bad is something I know without anyone telling me. Or perhaps I learned it so long ago that I've forgotten, and it's just become the truth.

Arranged around open squares, our buildings sometimes enclose a grass field, often with benches and playgrounds. Nearby, rows of clotheslines hang above concrete squares surrounded by prickly bushes. Two quads away are the showers where on hot summer days, water rains down on us from a tall pipe in the middle of a concrete circle. Children run around screaming, and grandmas wear their shower caps to keep their hair from getting wet. Mothers sit on the benches and gossip about each other.

Every corner of our square features a tree—two oaks, a crabapple with its hard green fruit, and a flowering cherry. Across Dayton Street are stables for the horses that run in weekend trotter races in the city park. In summer, the smell of steaming manure streams through our open windows. Across the other street, a church with a white steeple rings its bells every Sunday morning. The women going in wear hats and gloves and come out wearing smiles. Mystery happens inside that church.

Only women, children, and old men live in our projects. Like me, none of my friends have fathers living with them. I remember waking my father one morning—his head buried in the pillow, his skin warm. He smelled like cooked brown sugar. Maybe that wasn't in this apartment. In another memory, my mother handed me a pot of cold water and told me to pour it over my father's head. He leaped out of bed, roaring and sputtering. The projects aren't a safe place for fathers. That must be why we see them on weekends or during special visits. I never question this fact. It's part of being here.

These are the good projects because we can see the sky, and in the spring, a Japanese cherry tree with a name I can't pronounce blooms in clusters of soft, pink flowers. I climb up into the tree, surrounding myself with pink clouds. This is what heaven looks like, I think until white-haired Mrs. Adams shrieks at me from her third-floor window.

"That tree belongs to everyone," she yells. "Get down from there, or I'll tell your mother."

Like a jealous fairytale queen overseeing all her domain, Mrs. Adams is our tree warden, keeping nature safe from me.

"I'm not stealing it," I mutter so no one can hear me, but I obey. She will tell on me. All the lessons of my childhood are about obeying.

There's a routine to our life. The mailman fills a bank of nine brass mailboxes by the entrance door every weekday and Saturday. Keys jingle from the chain on his belt. I know the mailman's song about rain or shine and wonder why mail is so important. The milkman delivers to our door, the bottles cold and slippery in their silver box.

My father picks us up for an overnight visit every other Saturday in his used blue Pontiac with running boards. We call the car Bessie. Sometimes he sneaks in an afternoon visit in the dry cleaner's van he drives to pick up and deliver people's clothes. He gives us cough drops and drives us around the block. We sit in the back on the truck floor, and our hair gets full of static electricity from the clear plastic bags over the dresses. We don't tell my mother about those trips; my father has sworn us to secrecy.

The janitor burns trash every Tuesday. Even years later, I smell ash permeating the air when I remember it. Wednesday is our turn to wash the landing and stairs outside the first-floor apartments. We fold newspapers under our knees as we scrub and then spread them on the wet floor to keep it clean. We try to be civil to each other.

"We're all in the same boat," my mother says. I wonder what boat that is and where we're going. Sometimes I stand very still to see if I feel the motion and hear the engine's hum.

On the other side of our elementary school, ten blocks away, the newer high-rise projects stink of pee and blood. No one washes the hallway floors. Classmates who live there don't talk about their homes. Their silence tells me they are holding their breath. We have this in common. It doesn't matter which projects we live in; we all live by the same rules: stay out of trouble, keep your nose clean, be home by dark, or else. I've never tested what comes after the "or else." I don't want to learn.

The kids are too close to Butch, looming over him like oversized shadows. The sun is behind me, going down fast. Blond hair escapes their caps. I squint to see them better. One is a girl. They wear their dungarees rolled up at the bottom and unbuttoned cloth jackets over dark, knit sweaters. Carrying long wooden paddles, they tap against their legs in a kind of tick-tock as they talk to him, their breath mingles and hangs in the cold air like hot wash steaming on the clothesline in winter. The boy leans over and says something to the girl. Butch walks off toward his building, his hands in his pockets, without saying anything to me. He doesn't look back, and he doesn't wave.

"Hey!" I yell. "Where're you going?" I hold my arms out in the universal gesture of *What the hell?* although I'm not allowed to use that word.

Butch doesn't turn around. He keeps walking, his head down, hands concealed in his jacket pockets. Just watching him, I know something bad is going to happen. My stomach hurts. My mind whirls like a merry-go-round, and I look for a safe way to jump off. I don't question my assumption that I'm in danger. It's something I know in my gut. I know about danger the way I know what's good and bad.

There are two older kids and one of me. I'm eight years old, and they're at least thirteen and a head taller than me. That one of them is a girl doesn't reduce the threat. Girls here are fierce. They grow into it with daily doses of harsh words and punishment. We are all always angry enough to explode.

The kids at the bottom of the hill bellow, "Hey, you!"

I don't respond.

"Hey," the girl taunts again. "Irene. What a stupid name. Ur . . . ine, Ur . . . ine," she screeches, then folds in half, laughing at her own joke.

Butch told them my name. I freeze in my shoes. I know this is a betrayal without knowing the word. What else has he told them? What secrets have I let slip that will come back to hurt me?

Without moving, I work out my options. I could run along the top of the hill to the opening in the fence above the wide cement steps

16

leading to the street. But then I'd have to race the long way around the back of the buildings, past the clotheslines, past Butch's window. I'd have to run like a demon for three blocks to reach my front door. Their legs are longer than mine. They could easily catch me.

I could slide down the hill as if nothing were wrong and bluff my way past them, hoping *chutzpah* gets me far enough that I can sprint to my apartment before they block my way. That's iffy. And I'm not that brave. They're older and faster than me.

I remind myself they've probably thought of those escape routes. That's what they're expecting. I watch them for a few seconds. They've hunted a child younger than they are before, a child who's different from them, someone they expect will be weaker. The boy stands stock still at the bottom of the hill, waving his long paddle, waiting. The girl shakes her hips and makes faces at me. They're excited and confident, sure they can overtake me in half the time it will take me to get somewhere safe. I panic. This challenge is like one of those verbal arithmetic problems I can never solve in school.

My kitchen window is dark, but I know my mother and sister are at home, maybe in the living room watching television. If I can make it to the window, the closest I am to safety, I can call for my mother. She'll come to the window and scream at them. She's pretty fierce herself.

Head spinning, I leap and choose the kitchen window. I drop the cardboard and take off as fast as my legs will go, diagonally down the hill, away from them, and toward the building and the kitchen window. I don't look back. That'll just slow me down and make me stumble. I concentrate on not falling and get to the window. I'm right beneath it. I open my mouth and scream for my mother, but no sound emerges—not a squeak or whimper.

I try again. *Mom. Mom!* I scream in my head, but no one can hear me. My mouth opens and closes with no sound. *She must know I'm standing here. Is she punishing me for staying out too late?* I want to throw myself on the ground and cry, but there's no time for that.

The big kids are laughing even as they run toward me. They cackle and hoot, making fun of how I can't speak. They're just twenty feet away. I've got to run for it again, and I must go right by them to do it. I race for the next side of the building closest to my front door. From the corner, it's another hundred feet.

I almost make it, and then I'm up against the other new fence, six feet high and ten feet long, jutting out diagonally from the corner of the building, so we won't cut through the grass, because grass, like the mail and the tree, is important. I forgot about this fence. I look up. There are no windows on this stretch of the brick wall.

The older kids saunter toward me now, closer and closer, sure of their kill. I'm cornered by the wall and the fence. It's getting darker. The streetlights come on. I back up, thinking fast. My mother will punish me for not being in the house by dark, and I'm not going to make it. There's no way out of this mess.

Anger flares up in me. *I'll never talk to Butch again.* I hoard my fury for later, and my mind stills. I make a final assessment about these kids, about the possibility of escape. I can't win. *Don't let them see you're afraid*, I tell myself. *Don't struggle. You won't die from this.* I remind myself about turtles and pull in my head.

They move closer and swing their arms back from their bodies to get more thrust on the paddles. Small hard rubber balls attached to wood backboards by long elastic bands snap into the air and back against the wood. Their first few attempts miss me. They're aiming for my face and head, warming up. Hitting me is a game to them; I'm a moving target in a carnival booth. I put my hands out to stop the balls from smacking me.

"All you *kikes* is cowards," the boy says. His voice is so calm. He has blue eyes, a ski-jump nose, and a sneer.

I guess now what he said to Butch, who my mother calls "that colored boy." Watching her face when she says that, I learn there are people you hate, avoid, or look down upon based on rules still unknown to me, rules that never applied to me until right now. Now, these kids teach me, abruptly, like a scab ripped away from a wound I didn't know I had, that being Jewish is a color all its own, and that color determines who I can befriend, who I can trust. There's no point in telling them I'm half Italian. *Wops* are also despised. "*Jew-wopy*,"

I hear whispered in school hallways behind my back, delivered with the special scorn reserved for people who look like them but aren't, as if I tried to break into their club wearing a disguise.

"How'd you get in here, *yid*?" the girl says, her lips puckered as if she's tasted something sour. "Jews ain't allowed in here."

I almost laugh. She means in this housing project. *Where did she get this idea? Who told her this lie so long ago that it now seems true?*

"Good night, Irene," the boy sings off-key.

His sister giggles, her blue eyes blinking rapidly.

I realize they think only certain people can live in the projects, people like them, people for whom poverty is an affront because they're white. Living like this isn't how it's supposed to be for them; they need to blame someone else. Even at eight, I understand we all have one thing in common here, one special trait: we're poor as dirt.

My voice returns. "Cowards," I say softly at first as if sound is just trying out how to use my tongue and lips. "You're cowards!" I scream at them as their swing adjusts and balls begin to find their mark. "*And* you're stupid!" I yell for good measure, my hands curled into fists, my arms rigid at my sides.

Then I realize speaking is a mistake. Words won't hold them off. They're bigger and stronger, and they have weapons. I stop moving and tell myself to be calm. They'll have less fun if I'm calm. I crouch and cover my face and head with my arms. Experience has taught me that the attack won't last long. They'll get tired or bored the way my mother does.

They move in closer, whispering, planning how to hurt me, enjoying their triumph. Across the quad, a woman opens a second-floor window and calls out, singsong, "Andrew, Maria, come in now. Supper time."

Their heads snap up like dogs to the whistle. It's their mother. They live by the same rules I do. They must obey. They give me one last look as if to warn me not to tell anyone about this or to remember what I look like for the next time they're on the prowl and run for home.

I crouch on the ground for a while, working on not crying, although relief swells the sob in my chest. It could have been worse.

I check my pockets for a tissue and discover I've lost my mitten. Another small wisp of fear winds itself into my mind. It's too late to find the mitten now. I'll have to come back when it's light and retrace my steps. I stand up, dust myself off, and look around. There's no one in the quad except me. I walk back to my building in total darkness.

In the apartment, my mother is leaning over the bathroom sink, her head tilted back, tweezing her eyebrows into the thinnest possible arch over her eyes. "You're late," she says. Her voice carries annoyance, not worry. "It's already dark out." She glances at me. "Your nose is running."

I wipe it on my sleeve. My sister, sitting on the toilet, gives me a warning look, the one that means *don't say anything to flip her out.*

I was going to tell my mother about Butch telling on me, about being attacked by big kids, and then I thought better of it. "I lost my mitten," I explain. "I was looking for it." I walk into the bedroom, hoping that will be the last of it, that being home late won't be the last straw. Even if there's no reaction now, there could be a sudden explosion later.

"You're just going to the dogs, aren't you?" she calls after me.

I sit on my bed and hold my breath for as long as possible; my fingers curl around the blanket, and I wait.

SONGS MY MOTHER TAUGHT ME

My mother leaps from her chair at the kitchen table, knees clamped together, clutching her yellow silk kimono with the dragon embroidered on the back, and races to the bathroom. Her legs scurry like a spider's. Splotches of bright red blood leave a trail behind her across the floor. From the bathroom door, she shouts, "Clean that up!"

I wet half a dozen paper towels with water, wrap them around my hand so her blood won't touch me, and, shuddering, wipe sticky red spots off the floor. I turn my head away from the paper mess I throw in the trash and pretend not seeing it will protect me. I wash my hands five times.

This chore is as bad as carrying a dead mouse by its tail out to the incinerator and throwing it down the chute. It's not as bad, I learn later, as using a hanger to brain a mouse caught in the trap but not yet dead. Everything has its own degree of horror. I calibrate every act by its distance from revulsion.

I was five when I first saw my mother's sudden bloodletting and expected to find a blood-tipped knife at the foot of her chair. I made sure to sit as far away from her at meals as possible. Bleeding was a contagious condition for which there was no cure, a curse that might befall me at any moment. I could die from it. My mother knew what I thought.

"You wait," she said, confirming my fear. "It'll happen to you."

I didn't yet know I'd bleed regardless of my own volition. I was still young enough to think I controlled how my body worked—hands, legs, fingers, mouth—that it would do what I wanted when I wanted. I should have known better. I knew about threats; there were enough warnings. I should have taken her words to heart, but I was already dubious about everything she said. She was not believable. "Grain of salt," my sister would remind me.

I was still young enough to think that what happened in our home happened everywhere, that we were normal, and that mothers were universally unreliable. All families have something odd about them—something they hide, something that shames them. Our shame sat on my shoulders, and I was responsible for it, like cleaning up the blood, even if I didn't know what caused it.

Six years later, when I did bleed, my mother, for all her warnings, was unprepared. She wrapped me in old rags until husband number three could run to the store for sanitary pads. My knees were weak with shock that this was happening to me; I sat on the edge of the tub and waited. My mother mopped up the blood on the floor.

"You're a woman now," her husband said when he returned with the box. He smiled as if we shared a secret.

I averted my eyes and hated him for speaking, hated the shape of his lips making the words, the sounds coming from him. I pictured his tongue and tonsils wagging in his throat, which was more revolting than blood. I didn't want to have any secrets with him. Humiliation and hate bonded with the pain throbbing in the center of my body, stained by this new shame.

After my mother died, I found a photograph of us. The picture doesn't show two smiling girls leaning their heads against their mother's hips. Sarah and I pose on either side of her, each of us an arm's length from each other and her, wearing our best clothes—frilly white dresses, socks with lace tops, white shoes with straps. We don't hug. We aren't casual. We don't tilt our heads together as if pulled by gravity toward one another. There's no love in the image. We keep enough distance between us for a quick escape and wear a practiced grimace.

In contrast, my mother glows, leaning back against the flowering tree, her hands tucked behind her, flirting with the man taking the picture, a man we don't see—a man we never see, even in memory, erased by time or irrelevancy.

The photo reminds me of the lesson she taught me when I was nine.

"It's time you know," she said. "Photos with men are the ones you take to get dinner paid for. This is how life works, none of that baloney you see in movies." She twisted her head on her neck and looked over at me as if assessing whether I was ready to hear her wisdom. "Men are either saps or cads."

We were sitting at the glass-topped table in the kitchen. She had her coffee. I was drawing roses and swans with colored pencils on the pad of white paper my Uncle Willie had given me.

"Saps take you to dinner," she said. "You can hit them up for rent money or food. Maybe vacations, if you're lucky. The cads take you to bed, and while you're sleeping, steal the cash from your purse, empty your bank account, and abandon you."

Cads are the dark shapes of nightmares moving through your sleep, I thought. My crayon followed the satisfying curve of a swan's neck.

"Cads are the handsome ones, the charming ones who sing and dance and sweep you off your feet," she said. "Like your father."

The words hung sword-like in the air.

I was silent, clutching a rose-colored crayon, mentally erasing every feature of my mother's face so that years later, I had no idea how she looked when she told me this.

"About sweet nothings," she said, her eyes glassy. "Remember that *'nothing'* part."

I couldn't move, waiting for the next thing she would say. Breath froze in my chest. My face turned numb as if I'd been standing in freezing rain. My father was the one who warmed me, who kept me safe, whose hand holding mine was proof that I was okay.

In my mother's version of her life, she was the ninth child who trailed behind her older siblings and hid under the bed during her father's rages. Zuzu, the forgotten one, plain, dark-haired, dark-eyed with no special talent to snag her frazzled mother's attention. Her mother had no time for her; her older sisters couldn't wait to get out of the house. Her brothers, all except Willie, fled as soon as they could, as far as they could. They were poor, even by Depression standards; immigrants who'd lost everything except their lives and abundant fertility.

As if it had just occurred to her, she said, "The man you think is your father is not. He adopted you." She took a sip of coffee and glanced at me, watching my reaction.

Afternoon light slanted through the window and silently embellished the table's edge. Wrought iron leaves and grapes held up the glass top. I looked down and saw my feet. My mother was the one who taught me that the sky is blue and the grass is green. She taught me to eat with a fork and spoon, pee in the toilet, and how to put on my clothes. She was the one who named the world for me, who was supposed to tell me the truth of things.

"Who is my father, then?" I asked, while I still had words, while breath could still push sounds out between my lips.

She shrugged as if it wasn't important. Something in my head exploded with a bang that jarred my body. A red line threw itself across my paper. My face tightened; my legs weakened. I worried I'd slide off the chair into a puddle on the floor. I asked her again.

She shrugged again and raised her eyebrows to double the effect. "I was in the WACs during the war. He was a lieutenant. He shipped out and never came home. Uncle Willie introduced me to the man you think is your father."

Her face was a blank mask, as serene as a deep lake on a day with no breeze. I wanted to slam my fist into the glass, grab a shard, and shove the sharpest edge into her neck. I saw blood spurting everywhere, sprayed across the walls and floor. Instead, I asked, "Why are you telling me this?"

"I just thought you should know." She examined her red fingernails, then turned her head and looked out the window. "It's almost spring," she said as if we'd been discussing the weather.

I tested my lungs, filling and emptying them to see if I could. Even at nine years old, I knew she had an ulterior motive. These were words my father, who was suddenly *not* my father, gave me as a shield against her, even if I didn't understand them. She was manipulating me, another of his cautionary concepts. I knew when I told him what

24

she said, he'd explain she wanted something from me, something I wouldn't want to give.

Instantly, I understood what it was, what she burned to take away from me. Because *she* couldn't have my father for herself, she wanted *me* to let go of him—to hurt him. Like a jealous child, she ripped what mattered most to me out of my arms and barely blinked as she discarded it.

❦

In the last weeks of my mother's life, I hold up photos for her to see and point to images, asking, "Who is this?"

"I don't know," she says. "No one. I don't remember. It doesn't matter."

She makes me wonder if all the relationships we create, our links to other people, are so ephemeral that we can let go of them well before we take our last breath. By this point, I'm just a woman who comes to visit. She's forgotten I'm her daughter, forgotten so completely I wonder if I am. *Is there one more thing she needs to tell me, one last secret she's held onto?*

One afternoon, she recalls a man in a photo I hold up for her. "That's Sam," she states.

I remember Sam. He was short; his face narrowed to a sharp chin. He reminded me of a rat. He parted his black hair on the side and combed it over the top of his balding head. He limped and wore a strange shoe. My mother said he survived polio. He wasn't around long enough for me to care. He must have been a sap.

Or maybe, like the man who adopted me, Sam realized that if he stayed with her, she would drive him over the edge of his sanity. That's how my father explained their divorce to me when I asked years later. "She made me crazy," he said. "I would have killed her."

From the time I still napped in the afternoon, I remember incoherent yelling, the crash of plates on the floor, a door slamming, and then quiet. I remember reaching up for the knob, opening the door, and saying, "I can't sleep with all this noise."

My father, still my father then, carried me back to bed and said it was okay. "You're safe, Mouse." He tucked me in and kissed my head.

When I became a mother, I asked him how he could leave two little girls with a woman he thought was so crazy he might kill her. He shook his head and looked away. "It was so complicated."

Bedtime was my escape, a temporary reprieve from the constant alertness necessary to stay clear of my mother. I avoided having her tuck me in. The morning she pulled me out of bed by my hair taught me there was no safe place in our house.

Shortly after, I stayed with one aunt, and my sister went to another for six weeks. We never questioned the arrangements. My aunt served chilled cantaloupe before dinner and London broil grilled with slices of butter on top of it. She sautéed onions and mushrooms in butter and added red wine. This food was a revelation. She wore an apron over her dress and vacuumed and dusted her apartment daily. She told me that when I married, I should make sure we had twin beds so that I could get away from my husband. All these things I accepted as if I'd read them in the Bible.

I went with my father to visit my mother in the hospital. She was on the top floor, which I thought of as the roof. A brick parapet surrounded the patio where she sat, and stone gargoyles guarded the corners. Memory relies on vocabulary; I hardly had words for what I saw. I remember her in the open air, and when we got there, she stood, and I ran to her and threw my arms around her waist as if she alone could save me, as if she were all of love to me, and I'd been missing her.

Even as I hugged her, I knew it wasn't true. I was pretending, doing what everyone expected me to do. They expected me to love her; they expected her to care for me. But I knew better. She didn't care for me, and I didn't love her. I carried these lies along with the shame. They were somehow the same burden.

She tottered backward, and my father pulled me away. "She's weak, Mouse. Be careful." The visit was brief, and when we left, a sliver of the lie stuck sideways in my throat.

My mother came home from the hospital, and we returned to her. We wore clothes, picked the lint from between our toes, cleaned our fingernails, and slept in our beds. The public library became my safe place. I could walk there from home and went as often as possible after school every day. I sat in a polished wood chair and breathed in the smell of paper and ink. Everything in the library made sense; it was orderly and clean. I did what was necessary to keep this privilege.

At home, my mother left me notes: "Go to the delicatessen and buy bread, bologna, and cheese." "Start dinner." "Do the wash." "Pay the rent." She left me money rolled up in a napkin with the ends twisted. I had no idea where she went in the middle of the day. I walked to the rental office three blocks away and stood on my tiptoes to pass the money for rent under the grate. The woman gave me a receipt. I walked home singing to scare away bad people. The receipt went on the table to prove I'd done my chore.

One day, I came home from school, and my grandmother was sitting at the kitchen table having her tea with milk and sugar and a piece of rye bread with butter. Even now, the smell of fresh rye bread and butter is an intimation of heaven, rivaled only by the smell of cucumbers and sour cream. Those are the aromas of my grandmother's house. She brought them home to me, a small miracle as welcome as a fairy or a unicorn.

For a year, my grandmother and I did everything together. We hummed Strauss waltzes and listened to Dvorak's gypsy melodies on the phonograph. She told me fairytales about goddesses who made the world and read the "Psalms" to me. I believed her every word. When I came inside from the freezing cold, she tucked my icy fingers under her arms to warm them. I brushed and braided her hair. We shared a bed and the bathroom. I handed her soaps and oils when she bathed and helped her dress.

In daily skirmishes with my mother, my grandmother was my ally. "A *shanda*, Zuzu," she said, "a scandal." My mother escalated from slaps to brooms to frying pans. My grandmother said, "*Gott im Himmel*, do you think you make her stronger in heaven?"

My mother ignored her. Her eyes grew dark, her face turned red, and her fingers curled around the closest object. Sometimes there was time to duck, sometimes not. I had to be alert. No questioning was allowed, no objection. In my mother's mind, we were proving that she was in charge and her power was absolute. There was a method to her madness, she said.

"Are you crying?" she asked me through gritted teeth as if beating me was hard for her. She gripped one of my shoulders to get a better angle. "I'll give you something to cry about."

Years later, I realized someone in charge had said those words to my mother, over and over, often enough for her to memorize and speak them as if she'd invented the idea, as if it were perfectly normal to beat your child.

By eleven years old, I knew from her eyes when it was time to run as fast and as far as I could. I became an expert at dashing for the door. The day she chased me through the neighborhood, holding the iron frying pan above her head, screaming, "Come back here, or I'll kill you," things changed. The stakes were clear; I wouldn't survive if I stopped. Fear made me strong. Her fury ran out, and she went home. I kept going until I was lost, out of the projects, past the deli and the park entrance, beyond where I'd ever gone before and had no idea how to get back.

Houses I'd never seen surrounded me—white, brown, and gray clapboard houses with large windows, porches, and gingerbread trim. My mother had told me this was where the gypsies who steal children lived. I set my shoulders to be brave and asked a stranger for directions to the Seth Boyden Projects on Dayton Street. She stroked my head and looked at me carefully before she pointed and told me where to turn.

It was dark when I got back to the apartment. My mother had left the door unlocked but had no words for me. My grandmother gathered me in her arms. "*Shayna maidel,*" she said. Pretty girl. She stroked my cheek. I waited all night for my mother to get even.

And then, one afternoon, I came home from school and found my grandmother had gone as swiftly as she had arrived. I looked everywhere and finally asked where she was.

"I put her in an old age home."

Icy cold fingers snatched loose the part of me I reserved just for my grandmother.

My mother listed her reasons—none of her siblings helped her, no one gave her money, and Ellie wouldn't take her. "They don't care about me," she said, raising her chin and daring me to object.

I knew she was lying; she did it to rob me of the only one who spoke up for me, but I couldn't say it. An idea grew in my mind— what if my grandmother was not my grandmother but someone my mother made up to suit her purposes? The thought made me ache. I tested its truth the only way I had.

Eyes closed, I could picture my grandmother clear as day, her face lighting the moment she saw me, arms out to hold me. She offers me tea with milk and sugar and asks about my day. She spreads butter on a slice of rye bread and hands it to me. I have all the words I need for this memory. She will always be with me.

"You pay attention to me now," my mother said, her face contorted, poking me in the chest.

I turned away from her and wondered if, like my father, my mother was not my mother. My grandmother, though, was real even if she wasn't here, the comfort of her arms a blink away. "*Shayna maidel*," I thought and clung to the memory. "*Shayna maidel*," I whispered to myself before I went to sleep.

FINDING THE SQUARE ROOT
OF EVERYTHING

I lean slightly to my left and glance at Ina's paper. We both sit in the front row, and I need to be cautious. Mrs. Prince, our thin-as-a-wafer Latin teacher with double-lens glasses perched on her beaky nose, watches everyone. A bird of prey, her head twitches from left to right, up and down. I imagine her swooping down on me, putting her claws in my shoulder, carrying me out of the large window, and dropping me into the reservoir.

I know the rule. Cheating is a sin as black as taking the name of the Lord in vain. Nevertheless, I'm not above risking my immortal soul for an A. My heart hammers against my ribs. I hold my breath and turn my head.

Ina is wearing her customary below-the-knee, light blue jumper over a white cotton blouse with long sleeves. Nun-like, she shows no skin between her neck and toes. She wears white tights to cover her legs. It's 1960, and we're not allowed to wear slacks in school, but I'm sure Ina wouldn't wear jeans if her life depended on it. Even her shoes are buckled up. Her black hair is braided and wrapped around her head; glasses hide her brown eyes. Her skin is the color of rice paper. I imagine she's her father's delight and her mother's solace. I imagine great things for her. She's already first in our class.

"Eyes on your own paper," Mrs. Prince calls out from the back of the room.

If Ina weren't Jewish, I could see her in a white Amish cap. Perhaps one religion is the same as another, with strict rules that lock every normal woman into unquestioning obedience. I'm not normal; I question everything. Without our ever speaking, Ina knows I'm dangerous. I reek of difference—garlic and onions to her bland diet of boiled meat. She gives me a look of alarm and suspicion and conceals her paper with her arm. Correct answers are gold, and she hoards hers, not because she's greedy but because I'm not worthy— my cheeks flame.

Everything about me is a violation of Ina's principles. I'm wearing a red Banlon sweater that clings to my torso and a wrap-around skirt with no slip. Wind flirts with the edge of my skirt when we exit the building for lunch break. My dirty-blond hair hangs loosely around my shoulders and whips around my face in the wind. I go bare-legged and wear sandals as soon as it's sixty degrees outside. Boys look at me sideways, and I look back, daring them. Ina keeps her eyes on the ground.

In class, my panic over the past pluperfect eases, and I return my eyes to my paper. It will be what it will be. I either know this stuff, or I don't. When Mrs. Prince hands back my test the following day with an A marked in blue at the top of the page, relief floods me. *I can do this thing*, I think, *this business of learning*. Facts will penetrate the dense barrier around my brain and turn themselves in like model prisoners when I demand them. School is my safe place, a refuge for six hours a day.

When I'm sixteen, my mother goes on a cruise to the Caribbean with husband number four. My Uncle Willie stays with my sister and me for the week. We live in a single-family house with a driveway and a fenced backyard one block from our high school. We take garbage cans out to the street and get our mail in an unlocked box by the front door. It's a quiet street in the Jewish section of Newark. As the crow flies, we're five miles from the Seth Boyden projects, where we lived for thirteen years. Crows wouldn't dare come here.

"One wrong move," my mother threatens every few days, "and we're back there."

On the surface, we seem civilized. On sunny afternoons, I sit outside in the backyard and read the collected works of any writer I can get my hands on. To please the latest husband, my mother experiments with making *kasha* and other foods that taste like poison.

Sarah and I listen to Broadway musicals on the new record player, and my mother keeps the radio tuned to pop music on WNEW. The station serves up Sinatra, Bing Crosby, and Eydie Gorme. We learn all the words to the songs and develop a routine.

On the first night of his temporary guardianship, Uncle Willie makes a hash of hamburger, potatoes, and vegetable soup so delicious I have seconds. I imagine that when I live on my own, without my mother, all the world's flavors will explode in my mouth one by one. The taste of the sudden absence of acrimony, the easing of my body into sensation from its permanently rigid state, makes me realize I'm hungry.

Uncle Willie tells me about his upcoming solo show in the city. He has fifty canvases ready to go. He says the New Yorker published one of his drawings and hands me the clipping. A woman with a loopy flower in her wide-brimmed hat holds up her long dress to step over a puddle. She seems to be levitating. His name is in the lower right corner. I don't know enough to be thrilled for him, how rare and difficult publication is, but I pretend. He says his agent is managing everything. He just has to show up.

I grin. "That shouldn't be hard," I say, even though I know sometimes just breathing is hard, and good news is dangerous. Glee has teeth and will come back to bite you. I'm reading Greek tragedies and am doubly careful not to add to the weight of hubris already laid on the scales of our fate.

Talking to Uncle Willie feels like using a crayon to draw a line from dot to dot. I don't see the big picture. At the beginning of the conversation, I don't foresee danger. He tells me about an episode at the Veteran's Hospital during his last "incarceration," as he calls it. He's been in and out of the hospital since World War II—shell shocked, my mother says and rolls her eyes as if, had it been her on a muddy field in Germany under continual fire, she wouldn't have been scared out of her mind.

He was ambulatory and allowed to roam the halls, go to the common room to play cards, and eat in the cafeteria. Sixteen years have passed since the war ended, but he relives his worst moments in terrifying daytime nightmares. Sometimes, he acts out. He shrugs, telling me this. "It can't be helped." Shock therapy, he tells me, makes him into a zombie.

In his story, he saw the nurse with her pill cart in the corridor. He stopped her in the hallway and said, "You can give my pills to me now." He was being helpful, he says. She told him to go back to his bed.

He puts his hands on his hips, rocks his shoulders, and shakes his head, imitating her. "I'll give you the meds when I get to you," he says in a squeaky voice meant to mimic her. "Those are the rules. You're no different from any other patient." His lips remain pursed for a second as if the memory of her face and tone froze him in time.

Then he shakes his whole body with indignation and makes a face as he continues the story. "Hoity-toity," he says, meaning she's a snob. "And here I thought she was my friend."

I look down at the kitchen table and think about these phrases my mother and her siblings use—hoity-toity, hoi polloi—and wonder where they learned them. Years later, I find a sepia photograph of my Aunt Mellie as a child with her older brother, Igin, her younger sister, Allie, an unknown person, and my grandmother standing in front of a watch repair shop. The photo is from 1908. Mellie wrote on the back of the photo, "In front of our Havana shop with our servant." Somehow, the caption explains everything.

When I look up, Uncle Willie raises his chin and straightens his back. His blue eyes gleam. "I told that nurse that if she didn't give me my pills right there on the spot, I wouldn't move at all for the foreseeable future."

She refused to give him the medication. He turned to stone, standing rock still in the hallway, refusing to move a muscle. Orderlies came and carried him to his bed. He didn't move for three days. He nods at me, eyebrows raised, like a wizard to his apprentice as if to underscore how to pull off a great magic trick.

A small part of me retracts, sheltering me from him for safety. *Are you crazy if you pretend to be crazy and forget you're pretending?*

✺

At school, I enact piety in homeroom, reading the *Old Testament* before the bell rings, and speaking only when spoken to, the way I was taught. In class, my hand is the first up. My face signals *Look here. I've got it. Ask me.* I'm perfectly content when someone calls me a teacher's pet. My Spanish teacher says I'm a culture vulture. I see myself squatting on a dirt road, feasting on the entrails of the Roman civilization. My head jerks up as a vehicle approaches. My black eyes blink. Nero's legs dangle from my beak.

At home, my mother is redecorating, and everything is purple. Not a surface in the living room is free of decoration. She has found herself in this new occupation. Every day when we come home from school, there's a new pillow, vase, or chair. The drapes are changed, and the rug is new. Sarah and I go to our rooms and close our doors. I sometimes dream that she has dipped me in purple while I'm sleeping.

Her obsession doesn't last long enough. It ends the afternoon she accosts me at the front door, waving my underpants she dug out of the hamper. Three drops of blood stain them. The panties hang from her hand an inch from my nose. She jiggles them. Incoherent with rage, she renders me speechless, as if at a certain speed, sound waves break words into unspeakable particles. I understand nothing she's saying.

I take a step back, take a deep breath, and find my voice. "Just wash them," I scream back at her. "Then they won't be dirty."

The next morning, she's sitting on the sofa watching television when I walk by on my way out. "The bones in your ankles and knees stick out," she says as if telling me what the weather will be today.

Oblique assault is part of our war of attrition. If I don't rebut her, the invisible line marking my personal territory slips. I must defend myself. If I'm thin, it's because I can't bear to eat near her. The sound of her lips smacking together, her loud swallowing, and the way she chokes on her food without warning makes me sick.

But I don't say this. I look for the middle ground, the neutral territory, a place where facts might win. I hold my breath for a second. It's always a gamble. "Maybe my bones are bigger than yours," I say. "I'm taller than you."

She raises one eyebrow and nods. Equilibrium re-established. I am, in fact, taller than her and taller than all my aunts. When we're together, I feel like a giant redwood tree in a forest of dogwoods. Sarah is even taller than I am as if being born on a new continent liberated our genes from centuries of surviving in small spaces.

The next morning, my mother walks into the bathroom when I'm in the shower. She escalates. "What are those bumps on your nipples?" she asks when I step out of the tub. I know the tone. This is the beginning of a litany that will flay the skin from my bones.

I wrap a towel around me to hide the wound of my differentness. My knees weaken. *I'm not normal,* I can't help thinking. My mother keeps telling me there's something wrong with me, something that I can't fix. I'm never enough, always wrong about everything. She tells her sisters she can't manage me. She tells my sister that I'm poison. She says, "You used to be such a good girl," to me.

"Stand up to her," my father says, his version of affirmations ringing in my head.

I push her out of the bathroom. "I want my privacy."

After that, I always lock the bathroom door. She bangs on it from time to time, shrieking, "What are you doing in there?" I'm safer away from her scrutiny.

My mother's not interested in my grades. She mocks me for studying and moves my desk into the hallway, where she can keep an eye on me. It's a mutual suspicion. I wonder what she does all day when we're in school. She doesn't read. It's not cooking. If I'm not the one designated to make dinner, husband number four brings meals home from his restaurant, ready to eat. Afterward, he instructs me on how to clean the table and wash the dishes.

I snap. "I've been doing this since I was eight."

He reminds me of a bloodhound with drooping jowls and multiple bags under his eyes. I can't look at him, or my face will imitate my revulsion. I live for my escape to school in the morning, for weekends with my father away from her.

After dinner, Sarah and I sing our entire repertoire of Danny Kaye songs while we do the dishes. From the living room, my mother calls out, "Are you mocking me? I know what you're doing."

Defiant, we smother our giggles with our bare hands.

My mother brings up the subject of my ungainliness with my Aunt Ellie, the beauty. Ellie says if I lost ten pounds, I could model furs in her husband's store, rebutting my mother's assertion that I'm ugly and too thin.

But I'm still incorrigible and can't bear offers of kindness. I take five quick bites of the prune Danish Ellie brings to our house every Saturday. I love the white bakery boxes tied in red and white string, the smell of sugar that wafts from them, and the glaze on the eye-shaped pastry sprinkled with sliced almonds. I imagine I'm a vulture biting into the kohl-outlined eye of an Egyptian queen.

Lips sticky with sugar, prune still on my tongue, I can't stop myself from saying to Ellie, "I don't want to be a model. It's the last thing I want to do." I stomp out of the kitchen, ceding a triumph to my mother in the battle about how strange I am.

I come home from school on lunch break, open the front door, and my mother flies at me, her hands shaking wildly in the air, her face twisted. I have no idea what I did or how I failed her, whether someone died or we made a mistake and have to leave immediately. She screams and screams as if the world has ended. I stand in the doorway waiting for it to be over and notice the entire living room is now coral colored. Finally, she sits in the kitchen and breathes loudly enough for me to hear in the living room. I run out the front door and back to school.

At the first question in algebra, I burst into tears and dash out of the classroom, down the corridor, to the girl's room. I stand sobbing over the sink, unable to get a grip, no longer able to think about how "$3x^2y$" could be the radicand of anything or how it could possibly matter.

My math teacher, transformed into a bosomy, gray-haired grandmother, enters the bathroom and walks tentatively toward me. I watch her in the mirror. Her eyes are wary. When I don't bolt, she stands beside me and hugs my shoulders with one arm. She smells like baby powder. I want my grandmother.

"What is it? What happened?" she asks me.

I blurt, "My mother, my mother is crazy."

I'm telling the truth for the first time. Her craziness is the secret I'm supposed to keep, the shame my entire family keeps, never admitting it even to themselves. Keeping this secret is the root of every calculation in our lives, the core of the problem. Craziness runs in our family, multiplied across generations.

My mother's craziness is proof that I must be crazy. When I was little, I was sure that if I looked in the mirror in the middle of the night, I would see the witch who lived under my bed. At first, I thought the witch was my mother, but then I realized the witch would be me.

I don't know the punishment for telling this truth—fear spasms in my chest. I'm dizzy and nauseous.

My math teacher pats my back. "Rinse off your face with cold water. Come back to class when you're ready," she says as if these instructions solve the problem.

By the end of the afternoon, the teacher tells me to go to my advisor's office. Books line the walls. The chairs are comfortable. She tells me to sit. The principal called in my mother, she says. They've talked to her. An alarm blares in my mind and bangs down my spinal cord. I have no idea what she said to them. I have no idea if she was charming and persuasive or infuriated and insane. I bet on charming. She can pull the wool over anyone's eyes. I grip the chair arms and expect the worst.

My advisor, who is also my Spanish teacher, leans forward and puts her hands together in a prayer-like steeple in front of her face. "It's amazing how well you're doing in school, given what's happening at home."

My stomach unclenches. They believe me. I sit back and close my eyes. I breathe.

Two years later, I learned my mother told them my father was molesting me.

INCENDIARY DEVICES

I eat the whipped cream from my hot chocolate with a spoon. My date watches my lips as I lick them. Eyes closed, I savor the thick, sweet cream on my tongue. The city, lit for the night, romances the diner's windows. My date pays our check, and we run to catch the bus home.

Home is now with my father, who is *not* my father. He has a house with his wife, Eleanor, and her two daughters in a small town with a park, train station, and library at the end of his block. It's a new arrangement, and I'm still learning to navigate his world. In place of chaos, there are rules and expectations. That's okay. I don't want to sneak away from this house at night or run out the back door in the pouring rain, sprinting to a friend's home a mile away. I'm safe here. I want to be careful, to be good, to do the right thing. I want to stay. Getting permission before I act is required.

"Dad, is it okay to go to a concert downtown on Saturday with Siggy?"

My father looked up from his newspaper. "Where do you know him from?"

"He goes to my school. He's in the national honor society."

My father was skeptical. The boy might have lied. He suspects all boys of bad intentions. He used to be a boy, he likes to remind me and knows about these things. "Don't hold hands. Holding hands is making love," he says. "And never sit on a boy's lap." He lifted his paper and buried his head in it as if the conversation were over.

I don't know if that's permission or not. Even though it's been a long time since my father held my hand and called me Mouse, he's still a safe place where my heart beats out a steady rhythm. I wanted to convince him that this date was okay. "I met his mother," I offered as an argument in favor of the boy.

I didn't say I went to his home because I went without thinking after school and without permission. His mother is hugely pregnant with her seventh child. Her exhaustion hangs in the air, and sorrow inhabits every molecule of space in her house, like the smell of boiled cabbage and eggs. She was cleaning, getting ready for the Sabbath, and didn't stop to sit with me. She doesn't like me. I'm not Jewish enough. I didn't tell my father this; it's not an argument in my favor.

"You can go," my father said, his arms folded over, misgivings held close to his chest. "But be home by eleven."

On Saturday, Siggy comes into the house to meet my father. I introduce them. They shake hands, and Siggy bows his head slightly in deference. He's taller than my father.

"Nice to meet you, Herman," my father says without a hint of a smile.

Siggy takes his use of the wrong name as a joke and laughs. He doesn't know this is my father's way of classifying him—a species of will-o'-the-wisp, disappearing so soon it's not worth learning their names.

My father waves us off, saying, "Remember about curfew."

My stepmother watches from the kitchen doorway, gripping a dish towel, saying nothing. She lives in a perpetual state of knowing something bad is going to happen. Her expression gives her away.

After the concert and the chocolate, the bus leaves us a block from my home. Siggy suggests we walk in the park at the bottom of the hill. I nod in assent even though I know I'm close to curfew. We hold hands and walk along the lane by the creek. We talk about the concert, and I watch his face flicker in and out of the lamplight like an image in an old movie. The picture of him arranges itself without his permission, showing me who he is, hiding who he is.

He's not my first boyfriend. They come and go with the regularity of the Sunday comics. One day I'm completely fascinated by some-one and collect every artifact of their existence for my scrapbook, and then, poof, he's good only for lining the bottom of a birdcage. Even I'm astounded by how easy it is to discard them.

I'm a butterfly collector, attracted by the dazzling colors and pat-terns on their wings, unfazed by pinning them to a board where I can study their beauty. I paste their photographs and names on the pages and write I love them, but I have no idea what that means. They are trophies, the shine on their faces reflecting me.

This boy agitates me. I want to understand what I'm up against before it's too confusing to see where I'm going, and I get lost. I constantly list the pros and cons of loving him, comparing who he is with what's important to me. I have no idea if what I feel is love. My best friend doesn't have a boyfriend yet. We have no frame of reference.

I need an expert, but no one at home will give me a definitive answer about what love is. It's a dangerous subject. They pause, look down, and turn their heads away before they speak. Love is a secret so powerful that telling it to me would cause them to die. Knowing it would make me as powerful as they are or might make me free. Maybe the secret they conceal is that they don't love each other. In that fairytale moment where one person knows the truth and could change the future by telling it, no one speaks.

Love is one of those feelings I'm supposed to understand innately, like the difference between good and evil. It's the subject of every song and nearly every movie's plot. But I don't get it. When I ask my family about it, their sentences shorten. In a house of talkers, no one is willing to expound on this topic. I see in their expressions that asking about love is an act of sabotage. The word "love" is an incendiary device.

My father keeps his face in the paper and says, "You're too brutally honest," as if honesty were an act of violence. As if I would brandish it like a weapon if he told me the truth about love.

I sigh deeply.

He looks up, amused.

"Dad," I ask, "what does that mean?"

"Don't be melodramatic." He rattles his paper, dismissing me.

I ask my stepmother. She says something about contentment that makes no sense. If I were brutally honest, I'd tell her she doesn't seem content with my father, but I don't say anything. I don't ask my sister; I assume she's as clueless as I am. My stepsister says it's about finding "the one."

"The one who what?"

Exasperated, she gives me *Anna Karenina* to read, confusing me even more. Karenina abandoned her child for a guy with a mustache who lives with his mother when he's not riding horses, gambling, and playing with his sword. I ache all over for Karenina's abandoned son, who also must have had questions about love.

I flash on the image of a man with a mustache—the dashing, dark-haired, handsome hero—who used to visit my mother in the afternoons when we lived in a second-floor apartment on Schley Street. He turned out to be my mother's first husband. I asked her about him but lost interest when math proved he wasn't my biological father. Her marriage certificate to him was buried in her bureau drawer under her underwear in the same envelope as their divorce decree.

My mother said she was young, and he used to lock her in the closet so she wouldn't run away when he went out to play piano at nightclubs. "I just wanted to have a good time," she explained. I believed her then; she could be very convincing. "I was frigid," she also confided, as if that explained their relationship. I did understand this wasn't a love story.

My father, after much pestering, finally says love is action, more than words or a warm, squishy feeling in your chest. I'm more confused than ever. Karenina threw herself in front of a train. Is that the action he means?

I'm a scientist developing a hypothesis. "How do you know if you're in love?" I ask. I need a theory against which to measure my experience.

"You feel calm," my stepmother says. I know by her face that she's lying.

"You feel excited like you're walking on air," my stepsister says. "You can't eat, you can't sleep. You think about him all the time." Her blue eyes glow. I love her, but I don't understand what she's describing.

Over the phone, my mother says there's no such thing as love. "I'm moving to California," she says.

I'm asking the wrong person. I should have known better.

My father puts his paper down and looks at me. "Who are you talking about?"

"Nobody in particular. It's hypothetical."

He shakes his head and gives me a sideways look. He knows I'm talking about the boy who asked me to the concert. The newspaper raised, he picks at one whisker on his chin with his thumb and pointer finger, ignoring me.

In the park, it's dark between lamp posts. Siggy's thick hair covers part of his high forehead like a black cap. His eyebrows are caterpillars rippling across his forehead. Brown eyes, deep as a river, reflect the streetlamp a few trees away. He wears a silver mezuzah on a chain around his neck.

He leans down and kisses me. His soft lips taste like the sugar in my whipped cream. We sit on the grass, and his hand moves from my waist toward my breast. A small explosion radiates through me when his long fingers find my nipple. His other hand travels up my naked thigh. I suck in my breath.

I should stand up, be indignant, slap him, and walk off in a huff. That's what I'm supposed to do, although I don't know why I think this. But I don't stop him. *Making love is the adventure*, I tell myself, stepping willingly into the unknown.

Sex is over in a matter of minutes. I lie there, head ringing, small explosions going off in my body, wondering if I missed something or if I have miraculously changed. Rings of light circle the lamps. My fingers grope around in the grass for my glasses.

Siggy walks me up the hill to my house, kisses me, puts the chain with his mezuzah around my neck, marking his territory, and then runs off the porch and down the hill to catch the next bus to his home. He appears to be flying.

It's a little after midnight, and I missed curfew by an hour. My father waits in the living room, keeping company with the hands of his watch. He stares at the mezuzah on my chest. I wrap my hand around it and smile.

"Where have you been?" he asks.

I don't answer immediately. Before my father got custody of us this summer, I was a weekend guest who held her breath between visits. I'm good at holding my breath. I have years of practice. In the seconds before I answer, I consider what I'm risking.

This living room is as familiar as my palm with its brown couch, gold curtains, and two shelves of books over the television. Next to my father's recliner are his ashtray and glass of Drambuie neat. The tweedy living room rug is stained in places by the dog. Everything is the way it was before tonight.

This is your safe place, I remind myself. *Don't screw it up.*

The last time I ran away from my mother, she tracked me to my father's house and threw a metal trash can against the window. She banged on the doors and screamed, "You took my child, you stole my daughter!" until she noticed the new Chevy wagon in the driveway. "You have a new car!" she yelled, strangling on her rage.

She was in the process of suing my father for more support money. The lawyer she took us to see had a cramped, shoebox-sized office on the second floor of an old brick house in downtown Newark. His secretary's desk, surrounded by filing cabinets, was in the hallway by the rickety, wood stairs. He picked his nose while my mother talked and ate a candy bar as he asked us questions. He chewed with his mouth open.

My reluctance to cheat my father baffled my mother. I refused to answer the lawyer's questions. He pointed to the line next to my name on the long document and told me to sign. I wouldn't.

"He's not your father," she said, her face a pressure cooker with steam spitting from her mouth.

"Then he shouldn't have to pay for me."

"You're poison," she said to me. "Don't listen to her," she told my sister, the good child who signed the deposition attesting to the lies against her father, her real father, who loved her beyond definition. As a reward for her compliance, my mother took her shopping for bathing suits at Bamberger's.

I ran away, to the bus, to the house, packed my clothes and books, and called my stepsister. "I can't live with her anymore," I said. She didn't ask any questions, just picked me up in the old blue Plymouth with the running boards we called Josie and drove me to their house.

That night, my mother banged on every window of my father's suburban home on his quiet tree-lined street. She threw herself against the locked front door, then stormed up the steps to the back porch. My stepmother ran through the kitchen to lock the backdoor. My entire body shook. Flashing blue and red lights pierced the front windows and chased each other across the living room.

My mother shouted, loud enough for everyone on the entire block to hear, "He's not her father. He stole her. He's not her father."

A police officer came into the house, removed his hat, and spoke to my father in a low voice, examining his driver's license. My step-mother ran upstairs and brought down more documents. Papers rattled in her hands.

The officer turned to me. "Are you Irene Fermi?"

I nodded. I was sitting on the floor, petting the dog, pretending to be normal.

"Are you here of your own free will?"

"Yes, I am." My voice was as brittle as old paper.

He talked to my father, left the house, and took my still-screaming mother away. I stayed, my head whirling with the idea of free will.

The day we went to court, my mother stalked across the marble courthouse floor toward me, leaned in, her twisted face inches from mine, and said, "I hope you die."

Tonight, facing my father's disappointment, I wonder why I would risk doing anything that jeopardizes my place in this house. I silently rage at my carelessness, at the notion that any experiment would be worth the price of this safety.

"We stopped for hot chocolate," I say, telling a truth that's still a lie, hoping I'm persuasive, running a hand across the back of my skirt, hoping it's not stained green or that a stray blade of grass won't drift to the floor. "We missed the first bus and had to wait for the next one."

I try to think of what will convince him of my innocence. "The concert was awful. Baez spent most of the time tuning her guitar."

My father looks at me. His eyes accuse me of falsehood, but he doesn't say anything.

I wait and realize how easy it is to lie to him, a revelation almost as big as the notion of free will. The words fall out of my mouth as if they were meant to be said. He doesn't ground me. There's no lecture. With a start, I realize he's given up on me. The absence of punishment means I failed him. He expects nothing else. I've blown my safe world apart to find an answer to a question when the truth was right in front of me.

Sitting in his chair, he lights a cigarette, lifts the glass of Drambuie, and sips.

Years later, when I'm waiting for my son to come home well after midnight, I realize what ran through my father's mind while I was missing for that one-hour past curfew. He thought I was dead or mugged, left lying in a gutter, raped, robbed, beaten, and unable to speak. I was gone forever, his cherished child, and he would never see me again. And all this love, a treasure so profound he couldn't speak of it, the one thing he thought he would never find and did, would be lost without me.

CAT'S CRADLE

The single red rose wrapped in green tissue paper that I carry to give my mother before she boards a plane that will take her from Newark to California is deep red, half open, and smells of regret.

She's going to live with her sister, Mellie—the smart one, the lawyer, the one she always said she hated. On the phone, she explained, "There's no reason for me to stay."

Husband number four isn't a reason. My sister and I, fifteen and seventeen, are also not a reason. My breath caught for a second when she said that, and the thought burned like scalding soup as I swallowed. But I've been taught not to cry. Is this abandonment the worse punishment she promised if I did?

I was supposed to object, to say, "We want you to stay," but I never behaved the way she expected.

She has a litany of accusations. Every conversation with her is a revolving door from which there's no exit. I'm always looking for another way out. I'm to blame for everything, she tells me. I ruined her life. Inevitably, we arrive at her central question: Why did you run away? How could you do that to me?

I hurry through the airport parking lot, half running, thinking of an answer.

My mother sat absolutely still in the wrought iron chair at the kitchen table. Little metal leaves she painted coral—the same color she painted the blinds, the refrigerator, the walls, the table legs— pressed into the back of her white blouse. Her hands were in her lap. She stared across the room at nothing. Her face was blank.

"Mom?" I asked. "Mom? Earth to Mom." I was eleven. I waved my hand in front of her face. No reaction. She didn't blink. "Mom?"

I imagined her in the chair rocketing into the sky, orbiting the earth, sitting still precisely as she was, the chair making a turn around the world, putt-putting along, and then suddenly, in a whoosh, she jetted off into space, her feet dangling past Jupiter.

She had done this before, sitting and staring. I wondered what she saw in her head or if it was all black in there, like the lining of a dream.

After twenty minutes, I got fidgety. "Mom, do you need something?" Her chest expanded slightly and contracted; she was breathing. I was afraid to touch her. If I woke her in this state, with her soul flown away from her body, would she die? Could she re-enter her body? I was too young, these questions too difficult, and I had no answers to anything.

Waiting was the best option. I fixed her another cup of coffee, went to my room, sat on my bed, and read. After a while, I heard the chair move. I sat very still. When she came out of these spells, sometimes she was talkative and happy, and sometimes she was so angry I worried all the fixtures in the kitchen would lumber across the floor and leap out the window in fear. I didn't like to be nearby.

Neither my aunts nor Uncle Willie talked about her spells, but someone checked on us almost daily. I believed this happened in most families. Our door was unlocked. People walked in, there were hugs and greetings, she served coffee, and sometimes they brought goodies. These visits were the normal way of things. I saw it in *I Remember Mama*, my mother's favorite television show about immigrants making their way in a new country. My mother saw herself as the daughter, who was supposed to be a young woman. I thought of Mama as my grandmother, comforting me with kindness. But our family was nothing like the show.

I can't remember whether it was my idea to see my mother off at the airport or my stepmother's. If it's my idea, I got it from a sappy novel and already regret it. Worried the rose will wilt before we find her in the terminal, I hold the flower away from my body with two fingers—the green tissue paper around the stem crinkles. We stop to check the board for departing flights and gate numbers. Lost in the bustle of the airport, I let my stepmother be my guide. It's like flying blind.

When we find my mother, she's already standing in line, waiting to board. She's dressed in a red suit, stockings, and heels for her trip. Her hair is a shining helmet held in place with hairspray. She's wearing makeup. In my mind's eye, I see her spitting into the mascara case, rubbing brush bristles against ink, and applying black to her lashes. Her lips are bright red. I picture her outlining them in a deeper red, mouth slightly open, head tilted back in concentration.

I'm grateful my stepmother made me wear a dress and put my long hair in a bun. "Mom," I say. I don't touch her.

She turns around and takes me in with one look, and her mouth turns down at the corners. "Took you long enough," she says to me. She shows her boarding ticket to gate personnel and completely ignores my stepmother's greeting. "I'm almost gone." I'm too young to understand her agony, to see remorse in her imperiousness, to understand she can barely force sound from her throat.

I ignore how she snubs Eleanor. My mother has always hated my stepmother. She used to tell me how Eleanor came to our apartment to let her know she was going to steal my father. That was my mother's word, "steal." I doubt Eleanor used it. I doubt my father needed stealing. More like he was running away from her as fast as he could, and Eleanor had her arms out.

"She had some nerve," my mother said. "She sat on the arm of that chair." Her face twisted with scorn. She pointed to the green and white stripe slip-covered chair as if it were to blame. "She was wearing shorts. Her feet were practically bare. She swung her legs like a floozie." My mother's dark eyes burned, and her cheeks flamed. "It's a good thing I didn't have a gun."

I wondered if someone had a gun in her family and if that's what happened to her father, the grandfather who existed only in photographs taken when my aunts and uncles were young, the grandfather about whom no one spoke.

After my father died, I found a photograph of my sister's first birthday party. My cousins are in the photo, and my stepsisters-to-be. My mother is luminous, but Eleanor is beautiful. My father, who is not my father, couldn't help himself. Holding the camera to his eye, he saw the whole picture. Looking now, I also see how my mother saw it: the long-planned betrayal, lies, and secrets.

I offer my mother the rose, my skin drawing back from the heat of her tone, from how she's looking at me, making clear I failed her again. Words I might have said wither on my tongue.

"What am I supposed to do with that?" she asks. She glances at the matching carry-on luggage at her feet and waves the rose away. I hear the entire conversation without her having to say a word. We're in the part of our routine where I'm always wrong.

I pull the flower back to my chest. My breath catches. She turns her back on us, gathers her luggage, and walks to the boarding ramp. She doesn't turn around, doesn't look over her shoulder. My chest empties, and I feel smaller and taller at the same time, pulled in two directions, spineless.

There's no one to wave to, but I can't leave until the plane rises from the ground. I stand there, dry-eyed, in front of the wall of windows facing the tarmac, waiting to be released. If this is my punishment for running away from her, for choosing a safe haven, we're even.

Does she peer out of the window to see me watching? Could she even see me if she tried? I put my hand flat on the observation window just in case. I watch until every suitcase is loaded onto the plane and the passenger door is closed. The baggage trolley glides away, and the plane taxis to the runway, positions for takeoff, and speeds into the sky.

I picture her in her fanciest clothes, a gray tulle dress with sequins on the bodice. Did she wear this dress to marry husband number three? Is that when I formed this memory? She had her hair arranged in a red poof around her head. Sequins on the seams of her stockings glitter when she walks away. From the front door, she turns and says, "Take care of your sister. I don't know when I'll be back." I might be ten in this memory. My sister would have been eight.

She winks, grins, and runs out as if she were our older sister and not the mother charged with taking care of us. I lock the door behind her and drag the desk in the hallway against it. I turn on all the lights in the apartment. Sarah and I climb into her bed and pull up the covers. We read to each other for a while and doze off.

I wake when something runs across our feet. The second time, I sit up and watch a line of mice filing across the bed. I leap out from under the covers and chase them around the room. Dragging my sister out of bed, I close the bedroom door behind us and tell her to get dressed. The memory drops off at this point, and there's darkness.

When the plane lifts off, Eleanor says, "We can go now," and touches my arm. We turn away from the window that faces the tarmac and walk down endless corridors lined with huge advertisements. I toss the rose into the first trash can I see.

Eleanor drives us home. I watch the landscape change as we move out of the city toward the mountains and suburbs. My mother left without looking back, without turning her head. At seventeen years old, I'm an orphan, cast off without a sigh. *It could be worse,* I remind myself. *I could still be with her.*

When I was nine, my mother sent me with her boyfriend, the man who would be husband number three, to stay with him at his apartment over the weekend by myself.

"So he can get to know you," she said when I asked why I had to go with him.

She'd already told me that my father wasn't my father. Now that I was fatherless, I was supposed to love this stranger as if one adult male is as good as another fake parent, as if you can switch love off and on like the light, as if love doesn't matter. Or maybe it wasn't even about love. I was simply an offering, a proof of trust, a demonstration that she was willing to believe anything. I knew then he was a cad.

"This is a manipulation," my father, who was not my father, warned me. I told him she said I was a bastard, that I didn't have choices. He put his face in his hands and groaned but did nothing to stop her. I added my father's powerlessness to my understanding of saps and cads, my mother's categories for men.

"Why aren't you coming with us?" I asked her.

She shrugged. "I have to take care of your sister."

"Why aren't we all going?"

She never answered me. I heard her on the phone telling my father I had a cold and couldn't see him on the weekend. She winked at me as if I were part of the plot to deceive him. Standing there, watching her lie to him, I wanted to yell, "It's not true! I'm not sick. She's doing something terrible. Come and get me!" but I didn't. I understood his helplessness. We were all trapped in the same lie.

This man who wanted to get to know me had blue eyes, whistled frequently, was slightly balding, pudgy, and catered live television shows. He knew famous actors and took us all backstage to a comic's set at a television station in the city. People called him different names from the ones my mother told us. I wondered about a man with more than one last name and how he kept track of who he was. He lived in the Bronx, in a large building with an elevator and wide marble stairs. He held my hand when we walked up to the second floor and promised we'd go to the zoo in the morning. I asked where his children were. He said they were with their mother. I never met them.

He stood me on his bed and undressed me, shirt, pants, t-shirt, and socks. Someone in the living room was smoking a cigar. I heard men talking in that low grumble they use when they don't want children to understand them. "It's okay," he said, "They're my poker buddies. After you meet them, we're going to play cards."

He pulled on my panties. I held onto them with both hands. "These, too," he said. "Don't you want to be my good girl?"

I didn't. I shook my head. I didn't want to be anybody's good girl, ever. But he was stronger than me. "You're cute when you're angry," he said.

The following weekend he took my younger sister. I was relieved when my mother told me my sister was his favorite. "She does what she's told," she said. I was supposed to feel chastened, but I wasn't. I was incorrigible, the word my first-grade teacher had called me, the secret key to keeping myself safe. The thought made me smile. I never had to go with him again. It took my mother two more years—until he emptied her bank account and fled to Florida—to realize he was a cad.

Eight years later, I ran into him at the New York World's Fair. He seemed shorter, diminished, selling hotdogs from a vending cart, and wearing a white paper hat. I wondered what she'd seen in him. He blushed when he saw me and asked how I was.

"I'm fine," I said. I bought a hotdog and walked away.

My boyfriend asked who he was. "The way he looked at you," he said.

"He's nobody," I said. "Nobody who matters."

Eleanor pulls the car into the driveway, then puts a hand on my arm. "Are you okay?"

I nod my head 'yes,' then 'no.' I see she means well, but my mother's stories have immunized me against her. I push against the edge of the bubble around me and refuse to cry. "I'm fine."

My father wants me to call Eleanor "Mom." The word knots my tongue. I have no mother. The only mother I knew just left on a plane to go three thousand miles away from me, to "serve me right," as she would say.

Eleanor goes into the house, the screen door knocking against the frame behind her. I sit on the porch and stare at the cedar tree planted in the front yard in 1905, just after the original owners built the house. The clapboard house was fifty-five years old when my father and Eleanor bought it for seventeen thousand dollars. These numbers somehow calm me. The tree dwarfs the house now. I wonder if the older a memory is, the larger it is. I wonder if it grows each time I look at it. I wonder if I can stop looking.

Eleanor brings me an iced tea in a tall glass and sits next to me on the porch. This is another act of kindness, but I'm suspicious of kindnesses. My mother taught me that everything comes with a cost, particularly small victories.

The day I testified against my mother at the custody hearing, I sat dry-mouthed in the witness box. My hands were cold, my palms wet. My voice shook. I was sixteen, and I looked at the judge for instructions.

"Take your time, young lady," he said. "Tell me what happened."

The bailiff handed me a glass of water. The glass rattled against my teeth. My mother mouthed from her seat at the wooden table facing me, "You're poison."

I remembered a trip on a boat up the Hudson River to Bear Mountain. On the way home, my mother was furious at us for destroying her weekend. In the cab, she said to Sarah, "Why don't you just drop dead." We ruined her life, she said. We were selfish and annoying. At home, she ran a scalding bath and dragged Sarah off the bed toward the bathroom.

I was fourteen and tall enough to block her way. "If you do this," I said, my teeth locked together to hold in my wild fury, "I'll start screaming, and I won't stop until the entire neighborhood knows what you do to us."

She let go of Sarah and stormed out of the apartment.

I couldn't tell the judge about that. Instead, I told him about the night she came looking for me at my father's house, about her screaming when she saw his new car, about the trash can she threw at the window, and that she wanted my father's money.

My Aunt Alice, the good one, put her arm around my mother while I talked and stared at me as if I were an alien from outer space who had infiltrated her family. When it was her turn to testify, she told the court my father was a communist.

He was sitting in the front row on the other side of the court, wearing a tie for the occasion. He didn't flinch.

My father looks up from his paper. "How'd it go at the airport?"

"The way you'd expect," I say blank-faced, then go upstairs to change into jeans.

My room is half of what once was the master bedroom. My sister has the other half. I have built-in bookcases and a desk made from a door. I covered my bed with a hand-painted yellow batik cloth from

Indonesia. The walls are brown like my eyes. Not the deep, glossy, dark chocolate brown I envisioned, but brown, nonetheless.

My father has done everything he could to welcome us. The windows of my room face the tree in the front yard. There's room for an easel and a closet for my clothes. Yet, I still feel like an outsider, briefly perching here. This house isn't my native habitat; my species doesn't nest, and flight is imminent. My mother has shown me how. My father, not being one of us, is unsuspecting. This cage, he thinks, will be enough.

From my room, I hear Eleanor tell my father what happened at the airport. He curses; his recliner squeaks. He walks into the kitchen to make another pot of espresso. The water runs; I hear the soft crunch of metal against metal as he puts the pot together. Like a rite of passage to womanhood, we each learned how to flip the pot when steam spits out of the hole in the side.

Eleanor says, "Good riddance." The refrigerator door opens. "I'm glad she's gone." I hear a knife hitting a cutting board over and over. She must be preparing dinner.

My stepsister comes in and sits on my bed. "What are you reading these days?"

I shrug and point to a pile of books on my desk. I'm still not up to words.

She offers me *Cat's Cradle*. "This'll take your mind off everything."

I look at her and see how beautiful she is, how the whole world will welcome her with open arms. Her mother loves her. She knows who her father is. What does she know about anything?

"Shouldn't I think about it?" I ask. "My mother left me. She left us—me and my sister. She doesn't love us."

"Maybe it's not as simple as that," my stepsister says. "Maybe she thinks you don't love her."

I want to say something outrageous, something that flips the world upside down and changes the way everything looks. I want a new perspective that alters how the whole universe goes together, including me. "Maybe I don't love her," I say without emotion, taking the book.

My mother had made one attempt at reconciliation. She learned how to drive, got her license, and came to my father's house in husband number four's car to pick me up after school. It was the first time we'd seen each other since my father won the custody case in court. We went to Gunther's for ice cream sodas. I gave her driving tips.

I was calm for almost forty minutes. For a while, she talked about my hair and clothes, what I should do for my skin as if we were best friends, and I trusted her. I tried to be nice, but she didn't bring me up to be nice. I don't know the rules. I know how to do fierce, how to fight for my life, how to run. By the time she dropped me off at the house, I was hurling the brutal truth—the one weapon I have—at her. I threw myself out of the car and slammed the door.

"I ran away because you were hurting me," I yelled at her through the car window. "I ran away to save my life."

She drove off, and I stood there, tangled in the knots we made.

I turn *Cat's Cradle* over, read the back, and regret not keeping the rose for myself.

AURORA BOREALIS

My left hand, raised above me, holding a paperback novel, is missing my wedding ring. An indentation remains, ghost-like, on my skin, a reminder of allegiance and duty. My hands swelled at eight months, and by the ninth, the ring's gold edge cut into my flesh. I smeared my finger with butter and tugged off the ring. It sits safely in its box in my top drawer, waiting for my body to return to a normal state.

I've given up pacing the labor room corridor, bent in half, clinging to the handrail until each new pain subsides. Reading Dostoevsky's *The Idiot* between contractions, I realize I've lost my sense of irony. Words are dots I follow across the page. They lead nowhere and mean nothing. I shake my head at my lunacy. There are certain events from which you can't dissociate yourself.

I'm alone here. The nurse—in her mid-forties, short, round, and with abrupt hands—has gone on her break. "You're not going any-where for a while," she says before she leaves me imprisoned by her callousness.

Barred windows ride high on the two-toned walls in this old hospital's below-ground labor room—gray below the sturdy handrail and light yellow above. Fluorescent lights buzz overhead. The cement floors are cold on my feet. There's a drain in the middle of my floor. I won't think about what they wash away in this dungeon of my childhood nightmares.

Draped in a flowing green hospital gown, I can see my head and shoulders in the bathroom mirror. Expecting a transformation, I'm surprised I still look like me. By now, I should have grown wings, become six inches taller, and impossibly beautiful. My hair, washed in the shower when contractions were an easy-to-bear twenty minutes apart and two minutes long, is shoulder length. My brown eyes are raven fierce, my dark eyebrows like wings. My skin, normally what my father calls ruddy, is unusually pale, leached by pain. I close my eyes, avoiding my image.

Instead, I see the view from my mother's vintage 1953 blue Kaiser Manhattan on the drive along California's coast highway to the beach, hills on one side, open blue ocean on the other. Strangers passing me in current squarer models wave as if I'm somebody. I wave back, grinning, delighted by the momentary celebrity, and pretend I'm Elizabeth Taylor.

On this first visit since she left us, it's hard to be on guard, to remember my mother is manipulating me. The seduction of constant sunshine and palm trees unsettles me. I remind myself about the possibility of tsunamis and earthquakes, thousand-acre forest fires, and mudslides—the suddenness of natural disasters that plague the state—but glide through sunny days. I check out UCLA and consider transferring. I swim in someone's backyard pool in the moonlight and go on a date with my mother's friend's son. Over coffee with her friend in the kitchen, my mother plots a future I don't want.

But I'm beguiled until we go to Catalina Island for a weekend, and my mother disappears for a day and night without a word, leaving me stranded alone on an island in the middle of the Pacific Ocean with no money and no way of getting home. In the morning, she fetches me, her body shimmering with delight, and takes me to the yacht where she spent the night. The yacht owner tells me to smile, how pretty I am when I smile, and I remember why I ran away from her.

The day I leave, she dresses me in her persimmon-colored silk suit and does my hair in a beehive. Wearing the red high heels that match her suit, I look ten years older than when I arrived two weeks before, and she got me into Disneyland for the price of a twelve-year-old. We pose for a photo together.

"We could be sisters," she says.

I need a mother.

Pain hits, and I would rather be anywhere but here. I grip the sides of the bathroom sink and tell myself I won't die from this.

When I can breathe normally, I shuffle back to the bed and the novel, but my mind drifts. Telling myself not to cry, I lay the book down on my belly and close my eyes.

I'm suddenly fifteen and reading Alexander Dumas' the *Count of Monte Cristo* as if nothing else mattered. A train could have come through my bedroom wall and I wouldn't have moved. Transported out of my mind by delight, I called my best friend Ann to tell her what I'd discovered. Pacing the kitchen, wrapping the phone cord around my body first one way and then the other, I rave about the writing, the words, the phrasing. Pausing for breath, I tried to explain that I wasn't talking about the plot but the writer's method, how I could see what was on the page. I grasped for words I'd never said before, words I didn't know I knew, inventing language that would contain wonder.

"This feeling I have . . . this must be like love," I explained to Ann.

I talked for twenty minutes nonstop about the words, how he used them, and how they made me feel. I could see her shaking her head, blonde curls bobbing, rolling her blue eyes in disbelief. She listened, as she always did, but I suspected she thought I was a little cracked. She was right. Dumas split my world open, and possibilities leaked out. I would never be able to put myself back together, and I was glad.

Ann sighed. "It's a translation," she said. "Maybe those aren't the words he used."

She was a good friend, trying to tether my feet to the ground. She didn't need a story to transport her somewhere else. Her world made sense. Her parents' expectations bound her life. She'd go to college, get married, have children, and make a home for her family. Her life had a structure divided into chapters with a narrative she already knew. She could look around her to see her future.

I was plotless with a vague idea of what I was supposed to do, but no one had ever made it clear except to indicate they expected disaster at any minute. Each day, I wondered, *Is this it? Is this what I'm meant to do? Or is this the wrong thing?* My father always said,

"Look before you leap." My mother said, "He who hesitates is lost."
I balanced on the brink. Now, these words were vibrating on a page.
It's not about the plot, I kept telling myself as if those words were the
magic "open sesame." Even I didn't understand what I was saying.

I didn't tell anyone else about my love affair with a book until
years later when I gave my husband a copy of the *Count of Monte
Cristo*.

"This will open your eyes," I said.

He read it nonstop and grinned at me when he reached the end.
The story thrilled him. "What a plot." He grinned. "Revenge is very
satisfying."

You won't die from this, I tell myself as pain wells up, nudging aside
all else. *You won't die from this*. My distended belly is the height of my
bent knees as I lie on my back on the narrow bed. There's no one's
hand to hold, no one to console me, and I'm determined not to cry.

My husband is at his mother's enjoying the first night seder. The
nurse sent him away, saying it would be hours and she'd call him. It's
the late sixties, and she's in charge. Husbands aren't allowed in the
labor room. I gird myself for the fight with the nurse about breast-
feeding. I've memorized the words from the Lamaze book: "Don't
give me that shot. I'm going to breastfeed." I practice, speaking the
words out loud into the empty room.

This night, unlike all other nights, my husband is breaking matzo
and dipping it into wine. His family reads from the Haggadah about
walking out of Egypt. They say prayers and fill their cups with wine,
taste the bitter herbs, and savor sweet charoset. The Passover theme is
freedom from slavery and affliction. I skip over prayers and remember
hard-boiled eggs, apples mixed with honey and cinnamon, brisket,
and noodle kugel—my stomach gurgles. I haven't eaten for a day.

The phone in the nurse's station rings and rings. When I can't
bear the sound another minute, I roll off the bed, slip bare feet into
loafers, lumber into the empty office and pick up the black receiver.
On the other end, a male voice says to bring me to X-ray immediately.

Standing where the technician tells me, shaking with the effort
to remain upright, I feel water gush down my legs. It puddles on the

floor beneath me. "Oops," I say, gasping, embarrassed at the mess. An orderly bundles me into a wheelchair and whisks me to the labor room as my mind wanders.

We live in a second-floor apartment of a house immediately behind the playing field of my old high school. Just out of college, we have more books than furniture. An ancient Dodge Dart, a bed, a bureau, a bookcase, a round table and chairs, my easel, his guitar, and a trundle bed that serves as our sofa are our only possessions, plus the wedding gifts. No television. No stereo. It took an hour to move in.

Our landlord, his mottled forearm tattooed with concentration camp numbers, mutters, "You move like Boy Scouts," when he unlocks the door and hands us the keys. He must know what it's like to leave his home with nothing, to start a new life empty-handed. Later we learn he doesn't like the sound of two typewriters pounding away in the middle of the night. When his wife bellows at me the next morning, I notice the stamp on her arm. My breath turns sharp-edged inside me. I look at her face and guess her age. They must have been teenagers when they were in the camps. Blue numbers seared into human flesh change everything. My life looks suddenly easy.

We have so little money that each week, by Friday morning, we count out change to make sure we have dimes to call each other from phone booths if there's an emergency. After work, there's nothing to distract us except books. We read, play cards, and take turns beating each other at scrabble. We write words one letter at a time on each other's backs and guess the messages. We sing in the car, off-key, as loud as we can.

We wake on Saturdays to the banging of drums and the out-of-tune warm-up of the high school brass band marching on the football field ahead of the game. My husband walks to the deli and returns with salt bagels, a square of cream cheese, and translucent slices of lox. "On sale for thirty-nine cents for a quarter-pound," he says to excuse his extravagance.

This is heaven. This is everything.

When my stomach takes on epic proportions, we acquire a crib, a bassinet, a chest of drawers, and a baby seat. It takes four hours, but we assemble the crib twice—the first time upside down—and place it in our bedroom. We stand looking at the crib as if we've accomplished something important, our arms around each other, thinking this will be easy.

A nurse helps me onto the table; another bustles into the room. Their faces are no longer casual. The pain changes, and I must push; all my focus is on the pressure in my pelvis. I groan and remind myself I won't die from this. Then I hear a woman screaming in the corridor. My senses are alert; I change my mind. Suddenly death is a possibility. "What's happening to her? What's wrong?"

The nurse has her fingers on my pulse. "Don't worry about it," she says. "She's okay. She's a nurse." Her voice carries disdain. She removes the blood pressure cuff from my arm. "This is her third child. She should know better."

Her words don't reassure me. The woman's screams follow her down the corridor to the delivery room, and it's silent again except for my labored breathing.

Remembering the signs I read in the Lamaze book—the shaking, the urge to push—I tell the nurse, "I'm in transition." I use every ounce of my authority.

She's skeptical but lifts my gown and says, with barely suppressed alarm, "Oh, yes, I see the baby's head. I'll call the doctor. Hold on till she gets here."

She runs out of the room. I put my knees together and pant, dizzy with pain, and think about something else.

In the park, the trees were in full green. My bike glided on the path as my legs pushed me along in a steady rhythm. I stood for the hills to keep a steady pace and sat on the way down, letting gravity pull me. The road curved, and I leaned into it. Riding my bike was the closest I ever got to flying, and how I learned about freedom.

I closed my eyes and felt air brush my cheeks. My hair lifted in the breeze, and my soul expanded into the universe. I took my hands off the handles and held my arms out like wings. All the world floated below me. I opened my mouth, and sound rose from it.

When contractions are two minutes apart, and last ten minutes each, I discover pain has no boundaries. It doesn't stop at my skin, it fills the room. I pant faster. Sweat pours off me. I close my eyes, grip the bars the nurse has put up on either side of the bed, and try to obey her instructions. Pain is my entire world.

They move me to the delivery room, buckle my wrists to the table, and my ankles to the stirrups. The doctor gives me a shot of Demerol. She says something I don't understand about it being too late. The pain continues, but now I'm distant from it as if it's happening to someone else.

"Wait for me to tell you to push," she says. "Wait. Wait. Wait. Now. . . ."

I stand on the soft white sand at the beach, my toes in the ocean, my arms stretched out as wide as I can. The ocean sucks in its breath and sighs. Stars whirl above me in the dark sky. Water goes on forever. The horizon curves. For the first time, I believe the earth is round. I close my eyes. I want to embrace everything, to fill my body with it, to be it—the sound, the heaving water, the briny smell, the tiniest grain of sand under my feet.

I open my eyes. In the distance, ribbons of color undulate across the night sky. I look around at my family and friends. We're all seeing this. We stand stock still, our eyes wide, mouths open, watching the sky folding itself into green, blue, and yellow lights. This ribbon of colors, this extraordinary light, shouldn't be happening, but it is; we hold our breaths.

"It's the Aurora Borealis," someone says.

Everyone says, "Shush." We don't want an explanation. We would rather die from awe, our feet in the ocean, watching the sky change colors.

The doctor says, "That's it. You did it."

I wait, breathless, depleted.

"It's a boy," she says. "A boy," as if this is the first time in the universe's history that anyone has ever done something this astounding.

She places the baby on my deflated belly to cut the cord. Iridescent goo covers my son. *My son.* He squalls. I touch his head, his face, and something like God moves down inside me, filling every pore with light and changing every cell in my body. Light bursts from me, filling the room, the entire world, exiling pain. I open myself to it and feel weightless.

In the corridor, on the way to my room, the nurse uses the wall phone to call my husband. She asks me the number, dials, and holds the receiver to my ear.

It's morning now. He answers on the first ring. "You have a son," I say. In the next instant, I fall asleep.

When I wake in a hospital bed with clean sheets, spring sunlight glows through the window next to me. A vase of yellow daffodils, purple tulips, and blue crocuses sits on the bedside table. My husband, holding our sleeping baby now swaddled in a blue blanket, looks at me and beams. Light folds in waves around him. For a time, I am plotless, standing in the moment, flying, willing to die from awe.

SECONDHAND GIFTS

Uncle Willie arrives from New York City, limping slightly and carrying two bulging cloth shopping bags. His face is sweaty and flushed. He hugs me and asks for a glass of water. I tell him to sit, bring him the water, and delve into the bags he holds out for me.

One bag brims with a loaf of challah, an entire sleeve of hard salami, and a miraculously still-warm strudel from which waves of sugared apple and tart cinnamon waft. From the same bag, I pull chocolate-covered jellied candies in a flat box that slides open to dreams of childhood, and a dill pickle wrapped in wax paper. At the bottom, I find a piece of handmade jewelry and a hardcover book.

The title of this week's book is *The Territorial Imperative*. Flipping through the first pages, I see it was published in 1966, three years ago. Because the gift comes from him, I know instantly it's important in the same way I knew that Stravinsky's *The Rite of Spring* was critical to understanding the world when Uncle Willie gave me the record for my twelfth birthday. He knows things no one else in my family does.

He's stuffed his other bag with his sewing kit and pieces of folded cloth cut into perfect squares. While I watch, he arrays a kaleidoscope of colored fabrics across the dining table. Magically, the pattern of the quilt blooms into view. With no wife or children, his art is the center of his life, or so I think. I hover over the quilt, admiring it, thinking about him.

A little bedraggled, Uncle Willie wears an overly large, gray plaid suit jacket over a light blue short-sleeved shirt with an open, frayed collar. His slacks are a slightly different blue-gray plaid. I wonder if this is the new style. He shops in second-hand stores, my mother says. His fading blue eyes and thinning hair are the only fixed elements in a face that displays every emotion like a mirror of life taking its toll. It's hard now to fix a single image of him in my mind, except for his kindness and round cheeks, our family's genetic signature, the Hungarian in us. He's my favorite uncle, my own secondhand Santa Claus, savant, and storyteller.

He's been quilting for ten years. It's a more portable art than the painting he does in his studio. He must, he says, always be making something. His eyes twinkle as he tells me cotton is more malleable than stretched canvas. There is something irreverent in him, something that lets me know this act is rebellion against the role assigned to him. He quilts in restaurants when he eats alone and on the bus. His sisters are embarrassed by him. Women watch him, he says, and talk about him behind their hands. The glint in his eyes tells me he relishes his mild notoriety.

The bus ferries him from Manhattan, and he walks from the bus stop to my apartment in Irvington once a week on Thursday afternoons, just as he visited my mother in Newark when I was a child. I ask about his limp. He waves his hand, saying, "Don't worry."

I never comment on how far it is to my apartment from the bus stop or worry that it's a hardship for him to visit me. I never ask how it is that he isn't at work during the weekday or that, in his mid-fifties, he's unmarried and lives alone. He's always been alone. Now that I'm older, I assume heartbreak no one speaks about, heartbreak that is somehow normal and acceptable. It's not that he wouldn't answer my questions. Perhaps he even wants me to ask, but he's a natural phenomenon in my life, like a mountain or the ocean, the moon in the night sky. I don't question the moon.

His duplicate bridge partner, a physician in general practice, has a car and will pick him up at four before dinner, he reminds me before my husband gets home. That's part of our routine. He tells me this every week as if I might forget the arrangement. I try to forget nothing, knowing I inevitably will.

In my tiny kitchen, I inhale the yeast and honey aroma of the challah and cut thick slices for our salami sandwiches. At the table, Uncle Willie packs his pieces of cloth back into the bag and entertains my toddler, who sits in his highchair expectantly, watching everything.

Without any preamble, Willie turns to my son and sticks out his tongue. He presses his nose with his pointer finger, and his tongue slips back between his lips, hidden. My son stares, his brown eyes wide with wonder. Willie does it again. My son shrieks with glee and, with his small hands, bangs on the highchair tray to demand the trick again. Willie repeats. They understand each other, my son and my uncle. They don't need history, questions, or even words. For them, there is only now. And pure delight.

We eat our sandwiches and Willie quilts while I clean up, his fingers adept at pulling the needle through cloth in exactly the right spot, looping the thread, pulling again. His stitches are even, the same length, a marvel of precision. Repetition is mesmerizing. Pieces of cloth align in the growing puzzle to which he has the key. As he sews, he tells me stories about our family, the only relative who will and a violation of family rules. My elders guard a storehouse of unspoken secrets. It is *verboten* to tell them. Forbidden. These secrets are our treasures, never to be shared.

All my life, my mother has been telling me not to believe Uncle Willie's stories. The prohibition, I think, means he will tell me something true she doesn't want me to know. She rotates her finger in a circle near her temple, a gesture meaning crazy. He was shell-shocked in World War II and periodically spends time in the VA hospital, she says.

I nod, indicating I already know this. She persists, looking for the crack in my affection for him. She says they give him shock treatments, expecting revulsion, or fear, a fierce emotion that rips my love apart. Instead, I quake with sorrow.

Perhaps she means he's "crazy like a fox," her other favorite expression, as if truth leads us all on a frantic chase, escaping at the last minute from whimpering dogs that hound it to ground.

Willie never comments about my apartment, furnished sparsely in a style I call early relative, each mismatched piece flotsam from other people's homes. I've hung my prize possessions—framed prints of Andrew Wyeth's "Christina's World" and Picasso's "Mother and Child."

He doesn't care about appearances. He lives in a Greenwich Village third-floor walk-up, a dark, two-room garret where he's painted a mural on the ceiling. His neighbor, a fortuneteller, shares the hall bathroom with him. His eyebrows arch as he tells me this, as if there's something important in this detail and I should pay attention. I have his painting of the fortuneteller, greenbacks stuffed into her bra, looming above a tiny supplicant whose boneless limbs form a heart as she pleads for love. I wonder if she foretold his life, and this painting is his revenge.

He drops ideas into his conversations as easily as he puts sugar he shouldn't have in his coffee. He tells me about the plays he attends and the paintings he's making. "Do you know about surrealism?" he asks. He's been doing this—the subtle education of his niece—since I was a small child. He describes the delicious smells of ink and aging paper in the New York public library. "Old dust," he says, "has a flavor you can taste on your tongue." He changes my vistas. The world opens like a book I have only to check out.

This time, as he sews, he tells me about my Uncle Bobby, who drowned in the Pacific Ocean saving my aunt. Bobby, a year younger than my mother, was the last of my grandmother's nine children. He died before I was born. I recall Willie's portrait of Bobby. It hung over the purple velvet chair in my grandmother's apartment. To my eye, Bobby looked like Willie, but younger and muscled. I have the painting for reference and a photo album with black and white images of Bobby wearing a white jockstrap, posing on a hill under a bare tree. The photos shocked me with their boldness when I found them in a scrapbook under piles of another aunt's discarded memories. In the pictures, his body glowed in the early morning light—a young Greek god caught seemingly unaware in a moment of yogic contemplation of the horizon.

As in all large families, Willie and his siblings were given single-word attributes by their mother, a shorthand way to identify them in the developing story of their lives she would confide to her friends.

Bobby was the strong one, Hugo the handsome one, Ellie—Willie's twin—the beauty, Mellie the sharp one, Allie the good one, and Igin the smart one. Rarely did she mention Teddy, and Willie was kind. Zuzu, my mother, was forgotten, almost as if she were the secret they couldn't divulge.

"Bobby's life is a short story," Willie tells me while I change my son's diaper and put him on the floor to play. "He was eighteen, a bodybuilder hoping to make America's discus-throwing Olympic team. He went to visit Mellie in California." Willie checks his watch for the time. We have another hour, enough time for this story.

I imagine green palm trees, vivid blue skies, white sand beaches, and black cliffs high above a deep blue bay; the scent of flowers fills the air. Bobby and Mellie went swimming off a deserted beach in La Jolla and were swept away by a riptide. Exhausted from the struggle to stay near shore, Bobby held his sister's head above the water until the Coast Guard lifeboat reached them. Rescuers pulled Mellie onto the boat, but when they turned to get him, he was gone. They never found his body.

I imagine Mellie pacing the shoreline for hours, calling for her brother. I see night fall into the Pacific and Mellie, crouched by the edge of the surf, is the only one left waiting on the beach for Bobby to walk out of the sea. I see her returning home alone in her roadster, picking up the telephone, turning her back on the constellation of lights blinking on in the hills. She would have had to tell the story of how he drowned to Willie over the phone from three thousand miles away. I imagine the call, the operator connecting them, the strength it took to say the words, "Our brother drowned. Bobby's dead. They can't find his body."

I hear Willie say, "Not our Bobby. He was so powerful. That can't be. Are you sure?" The connection crackles; her weary confirmation fades. And then he told the story nine more times to his mother and each sibling, saying the words over and over until they were real.

Willie's voice is quiet. He stitches in silence. I observe the pattern developing across joined squares. He doesn't say the family grieved, ravaged by anguish. He doesn't say guilt plagued his sister. He tells the story as if it happened to someone else, as if it wasn't his heart that broke, as if his mother didn't weep for weeks. Perhaps that's the only way one can tell a story like that.

I watch my son, babbling as he plays with his blocks, think about what it would cost me to lose him, and close my eyes—a voice in my head howls. I recall my grandmother sitting in her velvet armchair under the painting of Bobby, crocheting antimacassars, her thoughts elsewhere. *How did she bear it?*

In my mind, I see her smile at me. "I bear it, *Shayna punim*, my cutie. I have you."

I look back at Willie. "You look like my mother," he says, half-reading my mind.

It's what everyone in my family says, even now. I look like my grandmother. They seem surprised, as if I should look like someone else. I don't mind, I tell them. As a child, Sarah was the spitting image of Ellie, the beauty. I understand my grandmother. Our genes circulate, retire, and re-emerge in endlessly reforming patterns stitched together by chance.

As an antidote to sorrow, Willie tells me about Mellie, the sharp one who didn't drown, and the story of her two husbands. One was smart, old, and rich, the other young, handsome, and reckless. She loved the reckless one and married the smart one. First, and when the smart one died, now rich, she married the one she loved. It sounds like a movie plot with Barbara Stanwyck in the leading role. I wonder if this is the truth or the story Willie prefers to tell. I wonder if there's a distinction or if truth is in the act of telling, not the elements of the story. Truth is not, I've already learned, always beautiful.

Years later, in the drawer of a desk my mother gave me, I find Aunt Mellie's 1923 diploma from law school. I add grit to the list of my family's genetic traits. I think of Magyars crossing the mountains on horseback to claim a kingdom. Yes, we could do that. I feel the horse moving under my body, spine to spine. I see the plain unfolding in rippling hills, a nation ahead of us to conquer.

My clairvoyance doesn't go very far. I don't see the despair, the loneliness, Uncle Willie never admits. I have no context to frame his sorrow. "None but the lonely heart," he sang on a record he made for my mother before he shipped off to Germany as a private two years before I was born. She played it for me when I was a child, wanting me to understand. Even now, the song haunts me.

At the appointed time, Willie packs up, gives me a hug and kiss, and limps out into the corridor. I watch until he's on the elevator, wave and close the door, and put my son down in his crib for a late nap.

A week later, Willie calls to tell me the doctors are cutting off his leg. "I won't be coming for a while. Gangrene has set into my foot. Diabetes," he says before I can ask how this happened. They can't take the chance that gangrene will creep into other organs. His voice is quiet and controlled. He talks about the surgery as if he were reading about it in a magazine. I call my mother for verification. But I should have known from the studied calm in his voice that this story is true.

I get a sitter for my son and take the bus into the city. I walk the thirty blocks to the VA hospital from Penn Station, glad of my legs, of the fierce Hungarian pride that pushes them along the sidewalks, of the grit it takes just to be human and survive.

I make my way through endless corridors smelling of urine-soaked sheets and the reek of hopelessness, find his bed, sit in the straight-backed visitor's chair, and wait for him to wake. Willie opens his eyes and smiles. He tells me about his stump. Doctors cut his leg off above the knee, leaving a flap of skin sewn back over the bone. He shows it to me. I call on every bit of courage I have and look at it with him. For his sake, I maintain an external calm, but inside, I weep and rage. *How can this be his fate?* I change his epithet in my ongoing saga of who we are: Willie, the brave one.

He introduces me to his roommates in the ward. "My niece," he says as if I'm a trophy he won for the highest score in a duplicate bridge tournament. I smile at everyone, showing them my grandmother's face.

KEEPING TIME

We slam through the double doors like a phalanx, ready for battle. They swing back against the wall with a cushioned thud. Our steps match, clattering on the hard floor. I want more sound, enough sound to split walls and echo in the halls, enough sound to shatter sickened cells and scatter their broken nuclei to the wind. But the hospital takes care of itself like a giant cybernetic machine, enveloping all intruders in hushed tones.

We stride through the employee hallway before visiting hours as if we belonged here but having forbidden access is no longer exhilarating. We're not winning. At the end of this long corridor, an old man slides down into one side of a wheelchair. An IV drips into his arm. His head has retreated into his shoulders. His blank eyes look like halls no one ever walked through. Saliva slowly wells in the corner of his mouth and drips down his chin. He appears to be the oldest, sickest patient in this waiting line.

They've marked his body with purple circles, like an ancient healing ritual to guide the Great Spirit. Without the benefit of magic chants, radiation technicians lower the machine intended to destroy the mutant cells that are killing him to no effect. It would be better if they sang.

Three weeks ago, at sixty-three, our father looked his age. Six months ago, he seemed ten years younger than that. Disease, like a cannibal, has eaten his time. We know the little that's left will be spent like this, watching him wither. We have to blame someone. The doctor long ago washed his hands of us. We blame the hospital—impersonal, mechanistic, Spartan. I imagine a motto inscribed in Latin above the doorway leading to his room: "Those who will live will live. Those who will die will die." I tell myself I must have the translation wrong.

＊

Sitting on the back porch of my sister's lake house, I write on a pad, "Yesterday my father died." He vaporized in the moment between breath and no breath, the energy that animated him blinking out, dissipating into thin air. A body still slightly warm to the touch remained, but my father—everything except my memory of him—was gone. Yet he's my father forever, even though he's not my father. For a time, I pretend to think about eternity.

Images fly at me. I picture him at my son's third birthday celebration marching around the neighborhood banging on a drum. Delight bloomed on my three-year-old's face as he followed behind, shaking a tambourine. I see my father five years later, the last time we visited him at home. He was already a skeleton with eyes like coals—huge, black, with hot red rims. My two-year-old sat in his lap, held gently between his bony hands. Both were speechless for a minute, the child matching this face with the one he used to know, the elder waiting to be recognized. We watched, not knowing what the baby would do. My older son wrapped his arms around my waist. We exhaled when the baby called my father Papa and kissed his cheek.

Did I tell him I loved him? In all those long months of waiting, in all those hospital visits, had I left that out? Before the coma, before his mind went, I told him about a conversation with a friend to whom I'd shown photos of us.

"She says I look like you." I grin. We know this is impossible; he adopted me. We don't share a single gene. At least, that's the story the family told me.

He smiles. "It's the eyes," he says. "They glow."

We know what we know, my father, who is not my father, and I. We know about love and longing and how there are never enough words or time or warm glances. I want to tell him he's my hero, thank him for saving me, and say anything that will keep him here. My throat clogs as it always does when I'm afraid, and I can't say anything.

The day after he died, my stepmother gave me his watch, the old National with the stretch band and the missing second hand he wore until the coma—as if time still counted, however dilapidated the instrument for measuring it. Stopped, the watch dangles from my wrist. Winding it won't make it keep time again.

I take it off and hold it in my palm. It's heavier than my own watch, not just from its size but from the accretion of time, as if all the seconds of all the years he wore it gave it greater density. As if the winding, wearing, and winding again accumulated something other than twenty-four hours at a stretch. Is it dedication, the doing again and again of the simplest tasks to keep going, that gives it weight? Is that all life takes? I shake my head and slip the watch back onto my wrist. I won't wind it. It's the most obvious metaphor.

This feels like a test. An endless line of teachers, eyes on the second hand of the clock on the wall, stands at the back of a classroom, and each takes her turn saying, "Time's up. Pencils down." I look down at my paper. I haven't filled in a single square.

My stepsister tells me that just before my father lapsed into the coma, he grabbed her hand and pointed to the newspaper she was reading. She gave him the paper. He stared at the front page, the headlines, the date—she didn't know what he was looking for, and he was beyond speaking—and then he closed his eyes. She watched him a long while after that and then reread the front page, wanting to know what had satisfied him enough to surrender. "He wanted to know what happened on the last day he was truly alive," she said.

Tomorrow we do the viewing. I have to be angry at something. I resent the required ritual. With no warning, I picture my stepmother reaching for my father across an empty bed, finding nothing, no one. Her imagined sorrow burrows beneath mine. Needing comfort, I call my husband to come to Jersey to be with me.

"I can't come," he says. "I've got the kids."

"Bring them. He's their grandfather. They should be here."

"I'm not bringing the baby to a funeral," he says. "And I don't want to leave him with someone else." There's an edge to his voice as if this conversation is about something else; we're speaking in code, and I don't know what the signals mean.

"That's ridiculous," I say.

Then I remember the day I glanced out the front window when he was supposed to be watching the kids. The baby, nine months old, wearing only a diaper, crawled on his bare knees up the asphalt street in front of the house. I dashed out the front door shouting, "What are you doing?" and sprinted seventy feet to the road, scooping up my baby as an oncoming car slowed. My son babbled happily in my arms, full of his first great adventure.

Face frozen, pulse pounding in my temples, I screamed at my husband, "What if he'd been hit by that car?"

"Well then, he wouldn't do that again, would he?" He rattled the paper and looked down at the sports page.

My breath stops, cold slices through my chest, the scene as fresh in my mind as the day it happened, and I realized I'd married a monster. In the next instant, I recall his mop of black hair, the comfort of leaning against him, and the space between his shoulder and neck where my face fits. I beg him to come to the funeral. "I need you," I plead.

"I have work on Monday," he says. "I have to go to work."

"You don't have to go to work. It's a funeral, for God's sake. This is your family. They give you time off to go to funerals."

"You're putting me in an untenable position," he says. When he uses words like untenable, I know we're no longer talking about a five-and-dime issue like driving two hundred miles with young kids in the car.

"Untenable position?" I hear my voice rise at the end of the question. "What does that even mean? How can you be in an untenable position? My father just died."

"Fuck you," he says as he hangs up.

I sob out of sheer frustration, and my stepmother insists I call him back. She stands in the kitchen and coaches me.

"You have to be at the funeral to honor my father," I say. She nods. "He was always good to you." She nods again, and I wonder where she gets her strength and why she would use it for this purpose.

My husband agrees to come for one day. I steel myself. There will be no comfort here.

"I'm divorcing him," I tell my stepmother when I hang up, discovering only at that moment it's true. She nods and walks out of the kitchen. That seems to explain everything.

Three days later, I watch him use a calculator to see whether he can afford a divorce. He takes an accounting of the value of our marriage as casually as noting the time.

After the graveside ceremony, seated between my stepmother and aunt from the safe distance of the limousine, I watch grave diggers lower my father's casket into the ground and shovel dirt on it. Everything inside me revolts. Burial cannot be the end of him, such confinement, all sight of him smothered. No wonder people believe in heaven.

As I sob, my stepmother says, "You wanted to see him buried, didn't you?" as if this act is her revenge for my loving him, as if erasing his physical being would obliterate it. I suck in my tears. There are many ways to tell a child you'll give them something to cry about.

I recall driving over a bridge so steep that the first time we traversed it on the way to the beach, I was sure we were all going to die. It went straight up into the sky—a long arching neck of black asphalt divided by a white line, its dragon's head hidden in the clouds. I imagined we'd get to the very top, the pavement would end, and our car would skid out into thin air and plummet into the river below. I held my breath until we were on flat ground again.

Grieving is like that and takes far longer than I expect. I can't see the end of it, and I'm afraid of where it leads. I remind myself that just because I can't see what's ahead doesn't mean life is meaningless and random, though I'm trending that way. There must be a purpose.

My sister taught me that. She was sitting on the living room floor playing chess with my father. It was the year she stopped brushing the hair on the back of her head because she couldn't see it. Dressed in his usual dark brown polyester slacks with a short-sleeved checked shirt over a white t-shirt, white socks, and brown lace-up shoes in which he also mowed the lawn, my father paced between chess moves.

"Life," he said, his finger pointed at the ceiling, "is meaningless."

She looked up at him. "Oh, I don't think so, Daddy," she said and made her next move.

He lowered his pointer finger from that invisible spot in space where emphasis lives, his face relaxed, and he smiled. "Really?" he asked. His head tilted. "Well, maybe not."

❋

At night, I dream of flying. It starts with the thought that I can. I spend one dream working to understand the physics, or engineering, of flight. I flap, run, flap, and jump. Finally, I realize all I have to do is will myself up, and up I go.

Then it's a matter of maneuvering, shifting my body, the way I would on a bike or horse, to move right and left, up and down. The next few dreams are about height, avoiding trees and roofs, and then one of simple ecstasy, soaring at will over hills and meadows, arcing into the sky, floating on my back.

I tell my dead father about this engineering feat as if he were alive. In my head, I hear him saying something about Freud's analysis of dreams. I ignore him. These dreams, I know without knowing, have something to do with freedom, with learning new things, achieving the unexpected, and being released from grief.

We have an early, cold winter, with snow before Thanksgiving and long into February, as if the earth is grieving with me. I fail at the simplest things. We run out of toilet paper. I can never find my keys. On three different mornings, I forget to turn off the car's headlights when I pull into my space at the Jesuit college in Baltimore, where I found work. At the end of the day, the car battery is dead. The first time, I sit behind the wheel weeping, wishing I could call my daddy to come and help me. Instead, I learn the first names of the men at the garage I call to jumpstart the car in the evening. I have three flat tires. A gasket blows. I feel as if my father is trying to tell me something in a language I don't understand.

Carl, the garage owner, fingers permanently blackened from grease, says, "You should trade in this old boat for something newer that won't break down so much."

He means to be kind, but he doesn't understand. A ton of steel encases my three-year-old son and me on the hour drive to and from Baltimore. It's our bulwark against harm. I shake my head; no, not yet; it's not time. I'm not ready for more change.

I wake in the dark. At the other end of the day, dark closes in early. By February, I've forgotten the color blue. I forget about the shapes of clouds, about what kind of clouds hang in the sky. I forget about telling the weather by looking and smelling. I lose the ability to forecast from the feel of the air on my skin. Half of my forgetting is from not seeing. I focus on driving, on dragons of black asphalt and white or yellow lines, on red traffic lights, and on green and white highway signs. I check in the rear-view mirror on my son, who sings songs to himself and stares out the window.

He calls out navigation markers. "Look, Mommy, the Baltimore cages. Here's the bridge. Look, look, geese."

One evening near home, I hear a bang and feel a shadow go by me, too close to the car. I pull sharply onto the shoulder. Face hot, adrenaline rushing, mouth dry, I look around, get out of the car, check the tires, look for dents. I check my son for injuries. There's nothing. We're fine. It takes ten minutes to catch my breath, not weep in terror, and convince myself I have enough courage to keep going, to do the next thing, and wind myself up so I can go again.

I worry that love is like time or money, and I'll run out of it the same way most weeks I'm down to my last dime before payday, the way unwound watches stop. I worry that the ability to love is encoded in our DNA—the way the length of telomeres signifies whether a life will be enduring or brief—abruptly ending when time runs out. What if there wasn't enough love in me to start?

Then I remember my father saying how he fell in love with me the first time he held me. "You were barely bigger than my two hands," he said. "You looked right at me."

I trick myself into thinking that doing things means I'm dealing with grief. On my commute home from work, I fight my way through five major highway intersections like a snail burrowing its way back through the chambers of its shell, all the while singing along off-key with John Denver about flying higher than an eagle. My son giggles in the back seat. He's the one with the musical ear. We stop at the market and make it to the driveway as the last notes of Elton John and Kiki Dee promise to love forever. I carry my son and the grocery bag inside.

Every light in the house is on. Standing in the hallway, my first-born wields my largest kitchen knife. I stop moving. "What are you doing?"

"I feel safer this way," he says. "It gets dark at six, and you're not home." He's ten and doesn't want to go to a sitter after school. I work an hour away. He's alone for hours before I get home. I don't know what I'm doing. I'm blowing this, and I don't know how to do any better.

I disarm him, hug his narrow body, and notice his face is thinner. I'm not feeding him enough, or he's growing taller. I hold his face in my hand for a moment, looking into his deep brown eyes. My boy is going to do wonderful things. I offer myself this consolation as an antidote to terrible parenting. I tell myself they will survive me.

"Mom," he says, "what are we doing about Jake's birthday?" He points at the baby, four years old this day, who's sitting on the kitchen floor methodically taking everything out of my purse one item at a time, examining it, and placing it in a pile behind him.

The question hits me like a dodgeball in the stomach. How could I forget his birthday? I pick up the grocery bag and put it on the counter. I'm not doing what I'm supposed to do. I'm the calendar keeper, the maker of celebrations, the ritual leader who says with food and gifts, my children matter. I've forgotten a red-letter day. These are the most important tasks, and I'm failing.

I look at my father's watch on my wrist and arrest my panic. I improvise. "How about you make Jake a birthday card from both of us while I do dinner?"

I have no cake, no presents. I'll put candles in bowls of ice cream. It's all I have to offer. I close my eyes and see my father holding out an orange segment for me, a gift of immeasurable pleasure I'll always remember.

It's enough.

"We'll celebrate this weekend," I tell him as if I'd planned it, actually believing it myself.

My son considers me for a second, his head tilted, then smiles. He collects paper and crayons from the drawer and sits in what used to be his father's chair at the kitchen table. Head down, he concentrates on drawing a multicolored whale with blue lines exuberantly spewing from the blowhole in the top of its head. More wavy blue lines along the whale's wide body indicate water. The sun is shining, and the whale is smiling. It's a happy day.

I put lamb chops in the broiler, start the water for noodles that I'll mix with butter and cottage cheese, and trim the broccoli—a feast fit for a king.

"Have A Whale of a Birthday," my son prints in red crayon under the whale's blue belly. When he looks up and smiles at me, I realize I have enough time for everything.

PREMONITION

Periodically I dream one of my sons has died and wake up sobbing. The dreams are vivid and involve blood and coffins. Omens fly up from them: locks in type boxes, thin men dressed all in black, a long dirt road, butterflies, shiny black shoes. I can make no sense of them. Dread follows me.

My sons are my home base, my win, my breath, and my proof of life on earth. We live on a tree-lined Baltimore street in our own sturdy brick cottage with two bay windows, a screened porch, and a fireplace. We have a dog too big for our small space, a lawn to mow, bushes to whack, and flowers to cut. We go to work, school, and the beach and strive for normal as if it's a place on the map I could circle and drive to if I knew the way. My younger son asks why I drive home a different way every time. I tell him I want to know all the escape routes. I don't tell him why. He prepares by memorizing landmarks.

I distract myself from impending grief with a lover—tall, broad-shouldered, whose lips taste like spun sugar and whose skin draws my hand against my will. I crave his breath in my mouth. Without ever meeting him, my mother is sure he's not my prince. She knows by what I don't say about him. She knows by the fizz in my voice, by my unspoken expectations.

She reminds me of what men are. "Saps and cads," she says. "Don't forget."

Like I need more proof.

He's the second lover since my divorce. I'm trying not to count. My mother knows about princes by proving their opposite through trial and mostly error. I worry I'm imitating her. At least I don't marry them. She asks me probing questions on the phone, and I provide half answers.

"Why didn't you marry the other guy, the Catholic?" She'd sized him up immediately. He was a sap, good marriage material. She should know; she's on husband number five.

I offer a complicated excuse and don't even understand why I'm telling her about this. Uncle Willie's death made me realize that life's too short for compromises. In the plus column, I tell her that this new man has a son. Our kids play together; he understands the demands of parenthood, not that she ever did. I don't say out loud that I know he's a cad. I'm ignoring that information. I don't tell her about the other compensations: the deep, luxurious sensations he evokes in places in my body I never knew existed. I make up the rest of him as if he's a story I tell myself. Memories of sex with him ambush me when I least expect them, and I moan.

After one year, I give him a key to my house wrapped in gold tissue in a box tied in black and white polka dot ribbon. He holds up the key, and it sways in the air like a leaf moved by a breeze. His face registers mild surprise as if he doesn't know what keys are for or what door it unlocks. As I watch him, a minor tremor, 1.2 on the Richter scale, rattles me. A metal taste coats my tongue. Something bad is coming. I know it, but my premonition creaks like hinges on an old box I neglected to oil, and I try to ignore it.

After a week's absence, he walks to the back of my house, where I'm prepping my small hibachi for a barbecue, and says, "Hey." He holds out two persimmon-colored roses and strawberries from his garden along with lies about where he's been.

My body reacts as if I'm allergic to him: my eyes itch and my skin prickles. I have to sneeze. I stop scraping the grill, and we sit on the screened porch watching the evening arrive, not talking. The sky slowly turns violet, then deep blue, and the colors calm me. With the kids at their friends, the house is silent.

As a salve to my itchy feelings, I say, "I want to make love," surprising even myself.

These words are a flawed translation of what I mean, leaping from my mouth and waving a flag in my face to alert me. I want to ask if he loves me, but I know that asking this question is a sign of surrender. The answer is binary: he does, or he doesn't. If he fudges, the answer is no, the response I don't want to hear. I should know better than to play this game; he's always one step ahead of me.

The rattan loveseat creaks as he shifts in his seat. "I spent the day with my son," he explains. "I have to work tonight, midnight shift. I want to save my energy."

I laugh, and again, my mouth utters words I don't expect. "I thought about cheating on you today."

It was a casual thought. I was lying in the sun at the Community Center pool and allowed a middle-aged man to flirt with me. He rubbed his hairy belly. Sun flashed hypnotically off his gold wedding ring. "You should say yes in life to everything," he said. I said no, but I took his card anyway; he reminded me of Agamemnon. I should have warned him about baths, but I didn't. I'm not Cassandra.

My young son, wrapped in his multi-colored towel, looking like Joseph before he told Pharaoh about impending plagues, gave me a look that said "Danger." For once, even in a dream-like trance, I listened. The boy can see things.

My lover gets very quiet. His face settles into a flat mask. I watch him for a minute, look down at his hand on my thigh, and look back up at his face. I take a deep breath and ask what's on my mind. "Have you cheated on me?"

He tries for candor. "I'm going to regret this." He lifts his head, looks at the ceiling, and sighs. "Yes, I have. But I don't see any point in telling you when or who. That would just make it harder for you."

My blood flows slower. I watch the porch floor contract in the cool of approaching night. I try speaking words. "At least I'm not crazy." I gather courage like blankets on a cold night. "Is it someone I know?" I bundle myself in bravado up to my chin.

"No," he says, his voice gentle, well-rehearsed. I wonder how many times he's performed this scene, with how many women. He's perfected his delivery. In a flash, the picture in my mind shifts. What if I'm the one he's cheating with? What if there's another woman somewhere who thinks he's her permanent prince? I hate the idea of being the other woman.

He puts his arm around me and pulls me to him, reaching to fondle my breast. He wants my head to nestle under his chin, but I am made of armor and bristles.

"Is it over?"

"Yes."

The thunder of his heartbeat tells me this is a lie. I fantasize about murder, castration, flaying the skin off his bones. *Survival, the brain is a survival machine*, I tell myself, pulling away from him, retreating away from the edge of the wall, away from where life drops into the abyss.

What comes out of my mouth next startles me as if my brain is operating under its own free will. "Would you check the light in the basement?" I ask as if we aren't talking about betrayal. "It's flickering, and I'm worried about a loose wire."

He thinks the worst is over. We go downstairs into the basement, where it's very cool. I shiver. He takes me in his arms, kisses me urgently, and pushes me toward the washing machine. His long fingers slide down over my buttocks. He slips his hand under my shirt, caresses my back, and cups my breasts. I feel nothing except a wintry cold snaking around my bones.

"I don't want to make love in the basement," I say, although the voice in my head screams, *Get out of my house. Get out of my life. Die on the way.* I pull away from him and walk toward the steps.

He looks up at the light in the ceiling. "Yup, we'll need to put in a new connector, maybe a new light."

I hear the "we" and snicker. He says he'd like to rest before he hits the road for work. We go back upstairs, and he collapses on my bed. I start to walk out of the bedroom and close the door. He calls me back and asks me to lie down with him. I climb onto the bed, which is suddenly too small, too high, and too awkward for anything like rest. He pulls me into the embrace I longed for, but now I'm a cardboard cutout, incapable of feeling anything.

He gives up in ten minutes. "Guess I'll head out," he says and swings his legs over the edge of the bed, the long muscles in his thighs clenching and unclenching under the thin fabric of his slacks. He pulls on his recently washed tennis shoes and ties them.

I don't ask him to call me; don't ask to see him. I don't say anything because talking would unleash the wild shrieking in my head. My quiet unnerves him. He hugs me hard, knocking the breath out of me. But the wiring's worn, and we're no longer connecting. He gives me a long kiss at the front door and leaves.

I collect my sons from their friend's house in the neighborhood, make dinner, watch a movie, and pretend I never met him. The boys know something's wrong without asking me. They give me hugs and tuck themselves in, hoping whatever it is will blow over by morning.

At midnight my former lover calls to say he's safe at work and I can go to sleep. The ritual reminds me of when I was six and how my father used to count to three before we hung up the phone. I put down the receiver and go crazy.

I want to destroy every vestige of him. I take down all the photographs, including the one with our boys at the beach, their faces bright with sun, salt, and sand. I gather up birthday, Easter, Passover, Mother's Day, Christmas, New Year, Chanukah, and for-no-reason cards he gave me, the notes I've saved just to have his handwriting, the sketch I made of him, all the gifts he's ever given me, and stuff them in trash bags. I want to set my bed on fire. Tears are no relief.

The sky turns gray, then white, and then it's morning. I climb into bed. My sons, ever resourceful, lean their heads into my bedroom from the doorway to say goodbye on their way out to catch the day camp bus. It's a blessing that I'm unemployed. I forget to worry about what my behavior teaches them and pull the sheet over my head, oblivious to what I've already taught them.

I consider the day. I think about going from seven in the morning to eleven at night awake and make a command decision. I'll take myself out to lunch, buy food for tonight, and briquettes, so we can have another barbecue to celebrate nothing. It seems important to plan my life. I lie in bed, procrastinating about when I need to get up and take a shower. I think about washing my hair and drying it, how I'll style it.

In the shower, I go over my wardrobe in my mind. I picture the clothes on each hanger and decide on the green-gray and lilac flowered shirt, green slacks, and amethyst and turquoise earrings. "Too many colors," my now ex-lover would say. *Heels? Oh, yes.* I want to look like a million bucks. In my mind, I change my shirt to the solid lilac-colored tee.

I'm slipping in the second earring when the doorbell rings. He stands at the front door with rolls of screening in his hands and a sheepish look on his face.

Hands on my hips, I stare at him through the window in the door. "What are you doing here?"

He looks taken aback as if we'd planned this, and I forgot, as if anytime he shows up at my home, I'm supposed to welcome him, that his telling me he was cheating was just an item from column B on the menu. For some reason, I open the door. He takes in my outfit; his eyes widen.

"I noticed last night the porch screen needs fixing," he says. "I thought I'd fix it till I got tired and then crash here for a while." Muscles in his jaw tense as he explains his unexpected offering of help.

I inhale the scent of coconut oil and sweat on his skin as if they were oxygen, and I've been living on Mars. I step back so he can bring his gear inside, but I walk away from him.

"You going out?" he asks.

"Yes," I call out from the bathroom. "The unemployment office."

"In that get up?" He sounds like my father.

I add layers of lipstick. "Yup," I answer, not giving a damn what he thinks, then press my pink lips together.

"Looks like you're going out to lunch somewhere." He's angry now, and the spark of it flies across the room.

I lead him into the kitchen. "While you're here, could you look at the pantry door? It won't close."

"What am I, the fucking maintenance man?"

"I don't know what you are or who you are. I don't know anything about you."

I'm screaming now, tears spurting from my eyes. Words cram the narrow channel of my throat. I'm my mother, full-on bat-shit crazy with no holds barred. I forget everything I ever learned about negotiation, about win-win. I forget my dreams. I want to obliterate him. I want my tongue to lash out and cut him in two. My shrieks summon dragons and fire. They can't arrive fast enough.

He takes a step back, horrified. "I'm not taking this from you," he says. "Nobody screams at me."

He walks through the kitchen to the basement door, opens it, and walks down the stairs.

I follow, still screaming, "How many times? How many women? Thirty? Sixty? Eighty?" as if betrayal has a calculus on a diatonic scale.

"Keep counting," he calls up from the basement. He trudges up the stairs with his bulging, black leather tool satchel under his arm.

This man is removing his tools from your basement, a little voice in my head comments, then giggles maniacally. I ignore it and bellow, "Oh, now you're leaving me. You betrayed *me,* and you're walking out, the victim, the aggrieved. You're the scum of the earth. You can't bear hearing the truth about yourself."

Teeth clenched, face inches from mine, he says, "I don't have to take this. You decide what you want to do. What I did, I did. I should never have been honest."

Oh, my god. He's done this before. Every. Single. Word. Well-rehearsed. Lots of practice. I'm such a novice.

He slams the front door behind him and walks to his car.

I sit on my bed for ten minutes without moving. His car vrooms off down the street. I recall my mother sitting at the kitchen table, staring into space, and for a second, I understand. I did think he was the maintenance man who was supposed to fix the broken parts of me.

"A cad," my invisible mother says from her chair at the table in my head. *"They always leave."*

Time passes. I stop paying attention to my dreams and switch jobs, move houses, cut my hair, change the color, and shed my skin. My older son declares he's going to ride a bicycle across the country with a friend. He doesn't ask permission. I hold my breath and think of him careening down roads through the Appalachian Mountains, unaware of careless drivers. I imagine eighteen-wheelers, pouring rain, tornadoes, and general catastrophe. I don't say any of this. To say it might make it happen. He needs his cloak of casual bravura to realize his dream.

He buys maps, and they design a route that takes them from Baltimore to Albuquerque. They roll four pairs of shorts and shirts into backpacks, fill collapsible jugs with water to strap to the sides of their bikes, and pack freeze-dried rations and a tent that folded is the size of a kitten rolled into a ball for sleep. He wears a Brooklyn shirt, and courage billows out from him like a flag as he rides.

The day before his trip, bicycling down a steep hill in a hurry to meet me at work, he smashes into the back of a suddenly stopped car in front of him, flips in the air, and rolls over the trunk, skinning his legs on the asphalt when he lands. As he tells me this, the word *OMEN* scrolls across the screen of my brain. I blink to erase it.

"I'm okay," he insists when I offer to take him to the emergency room. "It's just a scrape. My bike's fine." His voice is a practiced calm, honed over twenty years of managing me. He smiles. "Traffic around us parted like the Red Sea for Moses."

I look at his already scabbed leg. Misgivings flare in my mind like flashers set up along a dark road after an accident. He's teaching me to let go, but each new adventure leaves me dry-mouthed, empty-handed, and worried. I make him promise to call me when he arrives in each state. I try not to dream.

On the last call, they were in Kansas; a whole lot of flat, he says.

He tells me how a restaurant owner, impressed with their grit, gave them free bags of biscuits and sausage gravy on one leg of their trip. A motel owner let them swim in his pool. Regular folks offered the use of their backyards and showers. "After New York, this trip," he says, "restores my faith in humanity."

I hang on to his every word.

On the fifth week of his bike trip, nine at night, the phone rings, and I run to pick it up. My younger son sits forward on the couch and looks at me. The operator says the usual things about collect calls, but I'm not listening. I accept the charges and wait for the click to connect us. The voice is not my son's.

Fear heats my face. I stop listening as a crowd of crows takes flight in my chest. I imagine an accident. His friend has to call for him. I start lists in my head that will get me to where he is. I'm running through what I need to pack when words break through, and I realize it's my old lover on the phone.

I stop thinking.

"I'm calling from New York," he says. "I'm at a rest stop on I-95. I was assisting at the Six-Day, but they let me leave."

Who cares? You never could commit to anything. "Why are you telling me this?" My coldness surprises even me.

I look over at my younger son, who's now sitting at attention, watching my face, waiting for something. I smile at him, put my hand over the mouthpiece, and say, "It's just Dan." He knows who Dan is. He spray-painted the basement bathroom with black enamel to express his feelings about him.

"I'm calling about my son," Dan says, his tone measured out as if there's only so much sound left to him.

I recall seeing his son on his fourteenth birthday—tall, gangly, handsome—and how the word *DANGER* shot through me like a fast-acting poison leaving me weak. "Chris," I manage to say.

"My son," Dan says as if to remind me of their relationship, "is dead. He had an accident in the car I gave him for his sixteenth birthday. He was driving too fast and missed a curve. He hit a pole. He died instantly. I wasn't there. I was at the Six-Day. My brother called to tell me. I'm on I-95, maybe in New Jersey. I'm not sure."

I want to be calm when I speak and have no idea what to say. Saliva dries in my mouth; words abandon my mind. This morning, fog enveloped my car like a dream from which I hadn't awakened. Winding slowly through back roads toward the city, I watched it lift with no premonition of disaster.

I look at my young son—his soft brown eyes, that look of penetrating concern as if he were reading me—and think about losing him. A groan starts in my belly, travels up into my chest, and veers out of control, mapping all the places grief resides. I grind my teeth to hold the sound of it in my mouth.

I picture Chris at ten, all of us leaping for joy when his bat connected with the baseball. I remember Dan saying, "Did you see that? Did you see that? He's a natural." I see the boy dressed in a tux at a posh ceremony to celebrate his fifth year in remission from non-Hodgkin's lymphoma. In another memory, he sits on the couch with my boys, eating popcorn and watching a movie. He never asked for anything. I should have noticed his silence. I should have known what that meant.

"Do you want me to come and get you?" I know instantly how ridiculous that offer is.

"No. I'll be home in a few hours. I'll call you with the funeral details. I just thought you'd want to know."

He hangs up, and I sink to the floor, clutching my stomach. From between frozen lips, I squeeze out the words, "Chris is dead."

My son nods. "I'm sorry, Mom."

At the funeral in a packed church, Chris' best friend speaks into a microphone. "He's in a better place now," he says. "He's happier than he was on earth." The boy ducks his head and stumbles in his shiny black shoes back to his seat.

I cup my hand across my mouth and lean over my knees. Sobs spill through my fingers. I can't help myself. I cry for every child, silent in the face of fear, who pretended courage when what he needed was safety.

Long after the casket and mourners have filed out, I walk to my car, the only one left in the parking lot. I start it and pull out onto the street. Outside the church, Dan talks to a woman who smiles up at him, the tilt of her body inviting. He leans into her, touching her shoulder. A butterfly circles his head. I turn my car in the other direction and get lost on streets I know like the back of my hand.

My intrepid son calls that night from Colorado. The sound of his voice floods me with relief. "I'm worried about you," he says. "I had a terrible dream that two men broke into the house and hurt you." Two thousand miles from me, my son reads my feelings in his sleep.

"Oh, sweetie, it's not me," I say, slipping down to my spot on the floor. "It's Chris. Dan's son. He died."

He moans, his anguish opening another seam in my grief. There's no way to assuage this or make it easier. Regardless of how I tell the story, no matter what I say, this is how the world goes. Even if we're warned, even when we think we see what's coming or know a shadow lurks around the bend, we're wrong about the who and when—the how and what elude interpretation. The shock of each event reverberates over time and distance like ripples from the future's wake.

But I don't have to tell him any of this. He has the dreams, and he's way ahead of me.

FAILING

I drive up the rutted dirt lane, the access to a small farm off an otherwise well-kept paved road in an ex-urban part of the county that trends to large homes. My son sits next to me, tensely watching out of his window. On either side of the lane are sparsely planted woods of holly, pine, and rhododendron with no people in sight. We've time-traveled back thousands of years. I watch for shadows of people threading their way through the trees.

I'm moving us again, the fifth time in five years. We've gone from our brick cottage in Baltimore within walking distance to anything we needed to a fancy apartment building with a swimming pool. Then I moved us to a smaller apartment that flooded, and from there to a townhouse where we found a dead mouse under the stove. For a time, we nested in a house with half an acre of grass to mow and a view of horses in the adjacent fields. Now I've been riffed and can't afford the house anymore.

I recall the voice of the woman from ten years ago who called me after being laid off from Bethlehem Steel—the strained sound of imminent tears, anger torching the last of her civility—and know how she felt.

I joke that moving saves me from doing spring cleaning, but my son lost patience with me long ago. When he was fifteen, after I'd announced our impending third move, he left me a note on the kitchen table: *Just tell me in the morning when I leave for school where I'm supposed to go in the afternoon, and I'll go there.*

I laughed about it and admired his wit, but I wasn't smart enough to be worried about him, to pay attention. I told friends I was bringing him up to be resilient and didn't notice I was breaking him. Only his great humanity kept him from excoriating me. At the time in his life when I should have been present, when I should have been paying the closest attention, I was absent and so unaware I didn't realize it.

The lane opens to a cleared field with two large, clapboard houses on either side of a roundabout. For a second, his shoulders relax, and then a herd of pigs trots across the road. We stare. "Well, you've done it now, Mom," he says. "We really do live in the country." We wait for the pigs to pass. The pig herder raises his crook to acknowledge us.

The house is modern and pleasant, and he has his own room, though he's forced to share a bathroom with me. There's room for my oldest when he blesses us with a visit. We can move our furniture in, rearranging the family room, but this is the first time I've ever shared a space with a stranger, the first time the place hasn't been mine. Moving here is the closest I've come to homelessness, narrowly skirting the abyss, close enough to look over the edge and see the endless dark below.

It only strikes me much later that all this moving means something's wrong. I can't find my spot; home is the place I left in Baltimore, and nothing else feels the same. I dream of moving, of being forced to choose between decorated buildings and well-tended gardens, turning around and around in circles trying to make a nest, to get comfortable, and digging myself in deeper. Failure lives in every cell of my body like a cancerous thought. It metastasizes, affecting all my decisions. I can't get anything right. All my choices have disastrous results.

Every night I sit at the kitchen counter, smoking, and lay out Tarot cards. The Ten of Swords and The Devil keep turning up, no matter how thoroughly I shuffle the deck. The cards tell me what I already know: we're in danger here.

When words failed to penetrate my obliviousness, my son's resistance—at first a distant, low hum I could ignore—became action as if the energy of emotion compacted could become matter. First, I get a call from a truant officer, then from a store detective. "You should tell your son he's not cut out for a life of crime," the guard tells me.

I take that as a good sign. He stole a candy bar and a magazine. In the old days, this was called sowing his wild oats. I apologize, pick him up from the store, scold him, and take him to dinner, thinking, *well, that's done.*

Then a ratty chair with its stuffing held together by duct tape shows up in his room. I ask him where he got it. He says someone put it out with their trash. There's no reason I shouldn't believe him. Weeks later, I get a call at work from a police officer saying he's been arrested for burglary and I should pick him up at the county justice building. When I arrive, he's handcuffed to a table.

My face goes cold, but I'm still thinking about adolescent stages as if I knew what I was doing. We live in a middle-class community; the protection afforded us by our white privilege doesn't come home to me for years. He's not doing drugs or committing violent crimes. He has friends. He's going to school, learning how to play guitar. I'm too naive to be afraid. I am too blinded by my necessities. The county police release him to me as a minor; he won't have a record, but there's community service for probation and restitution to pay. I convince myself he'll learn something from this punishment.

He's calm and charming, contrite even. On weekends, we joke around, go bowling, watch movies, and eat out. I tell myself everything's all right; I pretend being handcuffed was enough to knock sense into him until he's staying out all night without a word, and I'm calling the police to report him missing. No longer a little child, he has to be missing for days before they'll look for him. The third time he does this, it hits me: he's imitating me, my behavior, the uncertainty he feels when I'm gone, and he doesn't know where I am. This is payback.

I try therapists, trainings, and beg his father for help, but nothing changes. And when an officer knocks on the door, shows me a fake ID, and asks if the person in the photo is my son, I say, "Shoot me now, and put me out of my misery," as if I were the one aggrieved.

The county chooses not to prosecute. There's no statute against stupid, the officer says. They're after the ID maker. I grounded him, but I've already grounded him for life twice before this. Why would he believe that punishment means anything? The minute I leave the house, he's out of the door.

I rationalize dragging him farther out into the boonies, away from the kids who taught or taunted him into doing things he would never have done before. I miss the boy I only had to look at to know what was going on in him, the child I used to sing to in my womb, the one I nursed until he was nine months old, the son who lit up the room.

I remember him at four years old, standing next to his older brother, who was kneeling at the front window watching for their father to arrive. "It's okay. He'll come," he says, patting his brother's shoulder with his tiny hand. "You'll see." Where did that boy go?

In a dream, I spiral downward, dragging him with me, and wake up dizzy and nauseous. At a shaman's afternoon session, my amethyst necklace is yanked off my neck by an unseen hand, and the purple beads scatter across the floor. I can't protect myself; how can I protect him from me?

I make lists to sort through endless details but never make headway. Time with my sons slips away from me, yet I'm heedless as if there were an endless supply of their company I could dip into whenever I needed it. Instead, I occupy myself with men who are no substitute, imitating my mother. I tell myself I have a right to life, that I won't find Prince Charming unless I hang around ponds and kiss a lot of frogs. The boys laugh, but my reasoning sounds hollow even to me.

My aunt dies, and her only daughter wears a leopard print shirt with a deep décolletage and a tight skirt at the funeral. She laughs inappropriately, and I know something bad happened when she was a child. I see how her mother failed to protect her and how her laughter covers a fury so hot it burns up her grief. I see how history runs backward and forward in endless repetition. Unless I do something different, my sons are doomed to repeat the same scale I'm playing over and over, even if they do it in a different key. Failure is built into me; I have to figure out a way to escape it.

I make every possible mistake. I find a note from my youngest begging me to pay attention to him and tuck it away with my precious things, but I have no idea what to do about it. I pray that whatever it is that saves us over and over from the worst outcomes will protect them from me.

My son stops being subtle. He crashes the car and, though seemingly unhurt, three weeks later drops to the floor in the gym, unable to walk. He tells me on the phone, "I can't feel my balls." I race to meet him at the emergency room, thinking of that other day so long ago when a car hit him, and I wasn't there.

Waiting for the emergency room doctor to tell us what's wrong, we sing Strauss waltzes—I hum the melody, and he does the bass. He spends three nights in the hospital, his head wired to an electroencephalograph machine. We leave with a diagnosis of concussion from his brain batting around in his skull when an oncoming vehicle crushed the side of our car. He had this accident when I was in another state three thousand miles away. We celebrate his release with pizza, and he gently reminds me that he doesn't plan to live with me for the rest of his life.

Within a year, I move again, and this time the space is small and cramped, but it's my own. He doesn't have his own bedroom; three rooms is all I can afford. I can barely manage rent and food, but I'm working and can see my way ahead. My anger at having no control over his behavior sneaks out of me in small ways—by refusing to cook meals and yelling at him for stupid things. Cramped in the tight space where we can't get away from each other, we're in constant battle, and, wrapped in willful self-righteousness, I snap at him when he has dinner ready when I come home from work.

It never occurs to me that removing him from his friends, the places he knows, and his routines wasn't the solution. He improvises to survive and I, working long days, am still blind. At eighteen, he escalates, steals a poor bloke's license plates, and we wind up in court with a public defender. I watch as he stands before the judge in the sports jacket I bought him for the occasion, my handsome boy, my gentle, funny boy, saying "Yes, your honor. No, your honor," and I weep.

It's a misdemeanor, and he gets another probation and community service. "Get a job," I yell, "go to college, or move out." I give him a deadline, never imagining how he hears that ultimatum—the abandonment, the rejection, how easily I slough him off—never noticing how he has to steel his heart just to breathe. And then there's silence and the icy glare of how much he despises me.

When I come home from the office on his birthday with a plan to take him to dinner and talk it out, the minute I open the door, a sensation of disorder stirs the air in the apartment. *Look for that which is missing*—the message from this week's Chinese takeout fortune cookie flashes in my mind like Morse code as I stand in the empty living room, dust spiraling in the late afternoon light from the tall window.

I scan the room. The collage I made with his photos, graduation program, diploma, and cap is no longer on the wall. His guitar is gone, his pillow, and clothes. I pick up my checkbook from the desk and flip it to the back. Three blank checks, the last three numbers in the sequence, are torn out. He's been an ace at forging my name on notes since grammar school.

The next day when my office phone rings, the vice president at my bank asks if they should cash a check made out to my son for five hundred dollars. The world tilts. That's my entire bank balance; it's the rent money. I'm paid every two weeks. At that moment when I have to choose between myself and my son, at that moment when I let fear vanquish love, I learn who I am.

I say, "No. Please don't honor it."

LEARNING BY HEART

I like long drives in the country on Sundays. Growing up in a city where grime was part of the landscape, I longed for clean streets, for more space. The goal is to wind up at a quaint, out-of-the-way inn for an early dinner. Maybe catch a glimpse of cows and acres of plowed fields, spot an unusual house, or drive through a town we've never seen before and stop to browse through its shops. It's probably a woman thing, this gathering of images to store away for times of visual famine.

So now, three years into a second marriage that adds my new husband's three kids to my two, we do that. We discover towns named Clear Spring, Huyett, and Flintstone, way out there in the country where you can't see homes from the highway without binoculars. The center of town is the local gas station, post office, and general store, all in one clapboard building where two worn armchairs wait on the store porch for those slow times when no one stops.

We drive past the Catoctin Mountains and out beyond Hagerstown. We drive to places where we don't know the names of the mountain ranges. We watch valleys get deeper and narrower. Mountains rise higher as we drive west, as if this part of the earth cut its teeth more fiercely. Rocky slabs of shale and sandstone jut sharply upward to form the Appalachians. From the air, this part of the earth must look like a tide of mountains frozen in the moment of crashing on the flat eastern coast.

We've taken this ride enough times now that my husband is in a rut. He likes ruts. "Ruts are good," he says. We know where we're going to make a pit stop, where we can grab a quick soda, and where we're going to eat an early dinner just outside of Cumberland, five minutes from the destination of every week's drive.

If we stay on the highway, it takes us slightly more than two hours to get to the state-run center where my stepson is in a residential drug treatment program. He's court-mandated there for ninety days, caught with our neighbor's collection of antique coins in his pockets and other items he's stolen to pawn for drug money. We're allowed to see him one day each weekend. We're allowed to call him for five minutes once a week.

That's not all, though, not by half. The State Police corporal who arrested him tells me we should have him checked for HIV. "The man who taught him these tricks," the corporal says, "the drug dealer, he has AIDS." The world is suddenly more dangerous than I ever feared.

On the day we go out to see our son, we don't talk much; both of us are lost in our musings, trying to remember to say what we've been told are the right things: "We love you." "We think you're a good person who got confused." "We want you to come home clean and sober." "We want you to be happy, to be successful."

These are the words we think we'll say before confusion and rage take us, before we lose our voices to sorrow, before the loud clanging disbelief that this could happen renders us deaf. We hold our breaths, clueless about the future. We're like the other parents who visit, groping for a lifeline to throw him so he can pull himself out of deep water. I listen to him talk. A quick study, he's learning the treatment lingo. I hope he's learning the words by heart.

An awakening began as subtly as light edging itself up over the horizon on a cloudless morning, bleaching the ocean to washed-out denim covering the lumpy knees of the seabed. In any day's first moments, anything can happen. Later, a sense of inexorability creeps in. It was like that when I found the first clue that something was wrong. That's how I put it to my husband.

"Something is wrong," I said. "Something's not right."

It was an itchy feeling, something I knew without knowing. I have no proof. Nothing has prepared me for this—not my wild youth, not my children, or my mother's stories. I have no tools to excavate the truth.

"I think he's been in our room," I say to persuade my husband to pay attention. "I looked through my bureau. Things are off kilter."

Vague intuition won't do. It's not enough, not by a long shot. *What was he looking for?* That's the question.

"You're imagining things," my husband says.

I point to odd behavior. He's in his room all the time. "Why do we let him eat in there?" I lost the battle with our teenagers for family dinners, a time they think of as cursed, each encounter a covert war where politeness is stretched tight over teeth.

"He's staying home sick too often," I emphasize. "He doesn't do his homework. He's staying up too late and sleeping too late in the morning. His room is disgusting. It smells like something died in there."

I go on and on until it sounds, even to me, as if I'm whining. My husband asks if I'm blaming him. *How can I tell him I am?* Our marriage is too new to sustain the truth. I bang away at his cave door for six months while the "Do Not Disturb" light blinks crazily. Then I give up and walk away.

I examine telephone bills. They're too high, by hundreds of dollars. The same number is called over and over and over at one-minute intervals late at night, the connection for one minute each time charged to us. I think, at first, the phone company's computer has a stutter. I point out page after page of telephone data to my husband.

"Whose number is this?" I ask. It's outside our area code, a long-distance charge to the same number more than twenty-six times in one month. Strings of calls to different out-of-area numbers are listed one after the other.

My husband shrugs. "He's a kid. His friends are in other area codes."

He doesn't see anything eerie in the strange compulsion to get in touch with someone, to find out something, and then to ask again one minute later. My proof fails. But by now, I know I can just wait. As inexorable as this process is, our awakening to it is just as inevitable.

✸

When we see Mark, he's subdued. He avoids hugging us until he checks out what snacks we've brought him. Then he tells us he's supposed to lead us through his "D'n'A."

I wonder if he means his genetic history and how he knows about this. Then he spells it out for me. Parents can be so dumb. He's talking about his drug and alcohol history, the complex double-helix of cause and effect, the twisted coil of genes, environment, experience, choices, and outcomes that landed him in this in-patient treatment center. His D&A. The blueprint of his future unless that magical thing called healing happens.

We are escorted into a counseling room. I scan my surroundings and note the wallpaper border: fishing rods, tackle bags, lures. I wonder if the counselor likes to fish or if he thinks this fishing theme is somehow disarming.

My stepson starts to talk. He says the first time he drank alcohol, he was seven. He tried LSD when he was nine. I feel responsible even though I didn't marry his father until he was eleven. My body goes numb. I'm watching a tidal wave move in from the horizon, and I'm unable to move. I stare at the fishing rods on the wallpaper border.

I glance at my husband. He's in the same state. We are waiting for the wall of grief to break over us. We say nothing. We saw the water move out, examined the barren coastline, picked up some never-before-seen shells, and ignored the tsunami headed right for us.

Then we ask a few tentative questions, testing our memory against secrets we would rather not know, the "This-didn't-really-happen-did-it?" questions. We ask to get clarity on things we think we know. Some things we ask just to prevent him from telling us more than we want to know. We are masters of denial.

In my mind, I'm making a list of people to kill, the people who led him astray, the monsters who abused him, but I feel guilty. *Where were we? Under what Everest-sized mountain of sand had we stuck our heads?* Pain bundles in my chest like a sack of rocks; the sharp edges have torn through the burlap.

I tell him I thought my job was to save him. He was always ahead of me, catapulting down dangerous pathways faster than I could reach out a hand. I tried to be vigilant, to figure out what he was doing and stop him before it happened. I failed.

I turn to face him. "I can't save you."

He looks at me cautiously out of the corner of his eyes; his head tilted downward. He looks down at his knees and back at me, full in the face. "I have to save myself," he says.

I can't tell if he really believes that or is just reciting the treatment catechism.

We leave early in the morning on our last trip to pick him up. Rolls of fog are stuffed between green mountain ridges. We pass each of the landmarks we've discovered in eight weeks of driving to the addiction treatment center, saying, "That's the last time we'll see that place."

This is a prayer.

"We don't have to go down this road again," we say together. We've had enough drives through the country.

We make a pit stop at Sideling Hill, where road construction ripped the cuticle off the earth's skin and exposed the raw flesh of eons long gone. There are no other people. We gaze out at the ver-dant slopes poking up through the mist that looks like white froth that tumbles up on a beach. Alone here early in the morning, we feel like the first man and woman transported to a time when trilobites made their small impressions in the rock.

We are at the center by 8:30 A.M. Mark paces the hallway, his bags packed, his goodbyes said. We have a last talk with his counselor and sign a contract with our son to help him through the transition from the complete safety of the center to freedom, the place where danger lurks.

In the car, driving down the long driveway away from the center, he says, "It's odd, but I'll miss that place." His voice catches. "The people who helped me, the routine."

I take him at face value, wanting to believe he's healed.

In the car, he talks about what he might do with his life, a conversation for which we've been yearning. We're convinced he could do anything if he just worked at it. He says he didn't know we thought that.

He goes straight to his room to make himself at home. Throughout the day, our other sons check in, in person or by phone. After each conversation, they say how changed he is, how engaging, how awake, and how present. "Was he always this way and the drugs obscured it or was he different?" they want to know. It's been so long, they can't remember.

A little of both, I think, looking into his eyes, seeing how clear they are, and discover, with a start, they're hazel. Drugs had disguised his eyes, his pupils chronically widened, the whites reddened.

At the dinner table, we pass the oval aluminum platter containing grilled steaks, bowls of steamed yellow squash and corn on the cob, the basket of bread, and the huge black salad bowl. Our prodigal, always the first to dig in before, sits back in his chair, arms folded across his chest, and regards the family.

"The blessing?" Mark mouths to me.

I nod yes, we could say the blessing. He asks if he can do it. His father, a catch in his voice, says yes.

"All blessings be on us," Mark says. "May we have love and peace."

I look up at him and wonder who he is.

We have a bumper sticker on our van.

For years I've avoided broadcasting that I want to save whales, human beings, or the planet, that we love our pets, chant "om" for happiness, prefer peace (mine) or war (his), and know Who's in the pilot's seat, or that we cherish the first amendment to the Constitution.

Now we have a yellow and black magnetic sticker that says, "Rookie Driver" we can put on any car Mark drives. You can read it from fifty feet away. We love it. He hates it. He's already forgotten that driving is a privilege we withheld for two years; allowing him to get this license shows that we trust him.

Trusting him with a car is like putting money into a market where the value of stocks daily imitates a steep and nauseating roller coaster ride. The ride leaves you breathless. I try to imagine him on the road, signaling when he's supposed to, coming to slow stops, pulling out of intersections without squealing the tires or whiplashing his passengers, avoiding trees, electric poles, jersey barriers, pedestrians, and obeying the law. Thinking about it exhausts me. I tell myself it's an exercise of will, the kind of guided imagery coaches advise Olympic athletes to do, but second-hand. I should have already learned I can't do it for him.

There's an added edge for me. When he's in the car, I won't know where he is, what he's doing, or who's with him. I won't know if he's hooked in and hooked up, using again until it's too late. This fear is my responsibility. His father has blithely skipped past fear into relief that his son is released and can resume a normal life.

Mark zipped by gratitude and zoomed on to figuring out how to simultaneously check out his hair, turn up the quadra-sound, and sweet talk an unnamed girl. I hope he has the other hand on the wheel. My fuse is short and his eagerness to get out on the road alone is enough friction to light the fire.

I wait for Mark to relapse. My anticipation is either a failure of will or horrible prescience. It's like waiting for hurricanes, tornadoes, monsoons, and tidal waves. I don't want it to happen. I'm terrified in advance and don't think the storm can be avoided. I'm helpless to stop it. My fear rolls downhill at me, picking up speed.

If you live in a region where natural disasters occur, there's a reasonable expectation that you will experience one. You buy hurricane lamps, reinforce the walls, and buy insurance, but no amount of preparation can make you ready for the moment when the wind growls, and the roof lifts off your house.

You live on the hope that when the flood moves through your town, rocks houses off their foundations, and leaves behind seven feet of silt and garbage in the living room, somehow you won't get hit. But you know from experience that near misses don't happen to you.

My husband is more sanguine or blind. He's in wait-and-see mode. He reads his son's lab reports and tells me there are no drugs in the kid's system. That is the fact. It's a momentary relief. Then I wonder whose urine Mark is using. My husband tells me that if relapses were viewed as the end of life, no one would ever recover. I see his lips moving, I understand the words, but I know he wouldn't say this if he weren't keeping the truth from me. A tornado is coming. I want to hide in the cellar.

Behind our backs, my stepson slips back into the murky world of drug use where up means down and promises guarantee nothing. I live on the boundary of anxiety as if it were a town I never want to visit, but I can't help noticing it's there. My path goes by it every day. *If you lived here,* the sign reads, *you'd be home now.*

I suspect everything. If a glass isn't where I left it, if the television remote is in a different spot than I remember, if the blinds are closed in the dining room when I return home from work, I'm uneasy. I go looking for answers, hyper-vigilant, the Sherlock Holmes of the mothers of drug-addicted kids.

I ask questions. I try to be calm, not to leap to conclusions before I have facts. I put information together, but I'm a great leaper. Something Mark says, the way his head is tilted when he says it, that his eyes are vacant, cause me to remember the moment. A collector of moments, I put that moment together with another until I have a rope long enough to strangle us both.

He rails against my not trusting him, and his father, in a pact to blame me, agrees with him. Somehow my not trusting him gives Mark the excuse for slipping.

I admit I don't trust him. "It will take a long time," I explain. "Stick to our contract," I plead. The littlest wrong turn, the smallest infractions, make me wince. "Don't go that way," I whisper.

Mark says, "You're making a mountain out of a molehill."

My husband sits between us with his head in his hands, mad at me, thinking I'm judging him. I'm cautious but believe in the utility of facts, even if this is the fissure that cracks our marriage open.

"I'll never be recovered," Mark explains. He's turned the language he learned in rehab upside down, making the concepts of chronic disease and relapse an accomplice to whatever he's planning.

I've become a meteorologist of lies. I watch the sky of our relationship for clues, check the shape and color of clouds, and notice the height of tides. I can tell by the way they move across my horizon that a storm is coming.

They used to put photographs of missing children on milk cartons. The large dark eyes, silky hair, and perfect skin of a seven-year-old child were embedded in an image on the waxy milk carton.

The photos always made me uncomfortable, as if that child watched me as I ate my cereal, accusing me of apathy. Often I turned the carton around. Sometimes I read the description. "Mary Ellen Rice, seven years old," it might say, "disappeared from her Boise, Idaho home on Aug. 8, 1980. She was wearing a brown sweater, a white t-shirt, jeans, and red sneakers. Anyone seeing her, please call this number."

Except, I'd realize with a start, it's now 1999. That seven-year-old would be twenty-six and look nothing like this photo, the last picture her mother had taken before she disappeared into thin air. She will always be seven for her mother, suspended for all time at the age of innocence. Maybe this was a last-ditch effort to contact the child herself, to say, "Come home, if you can, if you remember us. We will always remember you."

When my stepson disappeared, he took the 1990 silver Toyota Corolla his father bought him the week before, the hundred dollars in cash he earned for painting the shed light yellow, his one-week-old driver's license, his clothes, bulletin board, sheets and blankets, television and stereo, and the best pieces of my jewelry. He left a note on the counter in the kitchen saying goodbye.

"I'm leaving to find my purpose," the note said.

We spent two days in shock. We waited for a hospital to call, for a nurse to say, "We have your son here and need permission to treat him." We called relatives in California, our other sons. We said to everyone, "If he comes there, hold onto him and call us." No one called to say they'd seen him.

On the third day, my husband reported him missing. Then we waited for the police to call and say, "We have your son here. We're charging him with possession with intent to distribute." We waited for the worst, the unspeakable notification that he was dead.

We moved from shock to anger. We talked calmly about our options and realized we had none. I looked up the prodigal son story. It's a pretty good match, except for the ending. I hoped we hadn't had that yet.

Driving through town, I thought I saw him out of the corner of my eye. My chest clutched. I tried to plan what to do if I found him. I couldn't just pick him up and put him in my car. He wasn't seven anymore.

From the kitchen, I listened when my husband gave the police his description. "My son is five-foot-ten-inches tall, about 185 pounds with short, black hair, hazel eyes. And perfect white teeth. And he likes to wear vests because he thinks that's styling. He has a gift for telling stories like you wouldn't believe."

I imagined his picture on a milk carton and wondered if it would be twenty years before we saw him again.

My husband sat in his chair staring at the wall, remembering the child he loved. Images played against the backdrop of all his hopes. In his memory, he says all the right things.

WEDDING DANCE

I stand on the porch of a rustic lodge nestled at the edge of a state park, waiting for my mother. She's late. She likes to make an entrance, even when it isn't her event, even when all eyes should be on someone else. For five decades, she's relished keeping me on edge. I take a deep breath and wish for serenity. Inviting my mother to attend my son's wedding is like setting a place for the angry eighth fairy at Sleeping Beauty's christening. I should know better.

My youngest son thinks his Grandma Zuzu is the best thing since sliced white bread with butter. I learn this when he's twenty and finally works up the courage to tell me he hates pumpernickel, rye bread, and wheat—the kinds of bread I buy. Years before he had a license or a single driving lesson, she let him drive her car on dusty back roads past horse farms and wineries outside Temecula. He said she laughed out loud as he drove, even when he couldn't find the brake in time for the stop sign. He felt like a pirate, like a skydiver, like he'd won the lottery.

I remember her laugh. It always scared me.

My son reminds me that no one is only one thing. "She's brave, Mom," he says, his head lowered, voice soft, teaching me.

She's reckless with your life, flares through my mind. Anger rampages throughout my body, and I press my hands together to stop their shaking.

I shuttle between hope that she's changed and wishing my old bitterness would fade, weaving a cloth of grievances that grows every year. She didn't come to my oldest son's wedding or either of mine. I want this time to be different. I want her to live up to my son's belief in her. She no longer lives on the other side of the country. We're on speaking terms and can bear two hours in proximity. *Forgetting,* I tell myself, *is a reasonable path to healing.* I've taken training in letting go and surrendering, but something in me holds onto pain as if it's the one thing in the world that will save me. I can't relinquish it.

It's a perfect day. The air is crisp. Bright sunlight illuminates the restaurant porch decked out for autumn with hay bales, pumpkins, and abundant pots of yellow and orange mums. Inside, the space is transformed for a wedding. Music plays. Chairs are set in neat rows before an altar of flowers. Guests take their seats. Expectation bubbles in the air—we're all slightly drunk on happiness.

In fifteen minutes, my son will promise to love and cherish the woman who's chosen him. I remember pushing him on a swing. I see him playing with his lightsaber, riding his bike, and drawing at the kitchen table. At thirteen, he walks into the living room. "Listen, Mom," he says. Without looking at the page in his hand, he speaks in Hebrew from the *Torah* portion he's memorized for his *bar mitzvah*.

I put my hand over my mouth, my skin tingles, and my eyes fill. A heady mixture of joy and pride sets every cell aglow. *Kvelling*, a guest tells me at the ceremony the following week, is the word for this experience.

Today, dressed in a tuxedo, he's transformed again. I close my eyes and offer a prayer of gratitude to every god that holds us up. We made it across that unspeakable terrain when everything I did was wrong. Then anxiety ticks, and I check my watch. My mother's driving with my sister, but when Sarah's car pulls up with five minutes to spare, my mother's not with her. I ask why but don't listen to the excuse. There's no time for that. After a spurt of anger, like lemon juice in the eye, I feel relief. I pin the corsage ordered for my mother to my sister's dress, and we walk up the center aisle toward our front row seats as if we'd always intended this.

My younger son waits at the altar for his bride. It's a miracle we got here.

I remember the car accident when he was nine, the memory that still shakes me from sleep. I stand in a phone booth in the middle of the day, the glass door closed against the street noise, checking into the office from the road, and hear the receptionist say, "There's been an accident. Your son's been hit by a car on Park Heights. He was on his bike. An ambulance took him to Baltimore Suburban."

I'm connected to her voice through the black plastic receiver linked by a silver umbilical cord to the call box. She feels far away. Traffic rumbles by. I hear but don't register the words she's saying. No map in my mind emerges to guide me to where the hospital is. She tells me who notified her and who's with my son. My mind doesn't work. The story's complicated and involves my older son's friend and my ex-husband, and I can't understand anything she says.

This quake is a nine on the Richter scale. I grip the slim metal shelf in the phone booth to anchor myself. "Tell me again. I didn't understand you."

She repeats her message. My knees and hands shake. I take the pad out of my purse and find a pen. My vocal cords are made of shredded paper. "Tell me how to get to the hospital from Harford Road."

I hear her flip pages. "He's okay, Irene," she says. "He's not dead."

I take down the route she gives me street by street, turn by turn, thank her, and run to my car. Even if I knew where I was going, this would be a forty-minute trip. Time slips by—ten minutes, fifteen. I grip the steering wheel, wait for green, press the clutch, and the gas, shift gears, and watch for street signs. A red light traps me for five minutes that feel like an eternity. Baltimore is suddenly a continent wide and takes forever to cross.

Finally, at the desk in the hospital emergency room, I ask for my son. The admission clerk looks blank. For a second, I panic, thinking I've gone to the wrong hospital. I tell her what I know, "An ambulance brought him." I repeat his name. I tell her my older son is with him.

The light goes on. "Oh," she says, looking down at her chart, "they're in X-ray." She points to a sign above the double doors to her left.

I walk through the doors before she finishes talking, run down one hall and then the next, following the arrows to radiology. At the end of the corridor, standing outside another door is my firstborn, head down, arms wrapped around his stomach. He looks up at the sound of my heels on the hard floor and sprints into my arms.

We hold each other and sob.

"I'm sorry, sweetheart, I'm so sorry I wasn't there," I whisper into his hair.

When they wheel my young son back into an examination room, I take his small hand in mine, brush the hair from his pale face, and kiss his cheek. I have no idea where I can touch him, where there will be no pain.

"My brave boy," I say, helpless, guilty, then empty of everything but gratitude that he's alive.

The doctor pats my shoulder. "You have great kids," he says. He searches my eyes to find a clue that explains this. "I've never seen anything like it, the way they relate to each other."

I can't speak and hug my secret knowledge that they came this way. How could I ever explain that they comfort me every day?

The doctor tells me about a leg cast and keeping my son bed bound. Two tons of steel hit him as he rode his bike in the street, and the bone that broke was his knee. There's no concussion, no internal bleeding, and no ruptured spleen. I wait to hear the doctor say, "Your son can go home."

While he talks, I imagine my boy hit by the car, thrown head over heels into the air, smashing down against the windshield, sliding to the ground, lying there, without me. I imagine his fear, the sirens, see the EMTs, and suck in my breath. I push him out of the hospital in a wheelchair, knowing I owe something for this miracle.

Now here he is, holding his bride's hands. Light shines from his face. The bride smiles at him. *He did it.* For a second, I understand the leap of faith that love is. They each say, "I do," and a sob dances in my chest. Their vows complete, my son and new daughter turn toward our applause. We throw bouquets of happily-ever-afters, shower them with blessings, and promise everything good forever. We assemble for photographs, and I blink in the flash. It's just as well that my mother's not here.

Rooting around in the attic of her mind, she would've found one of my failures and flung it at me, her comment delivered in her most gift-wrapped voice. "That house is bigger than yours." "I knew your first marriage would end when I saw that photo of you sitting on the floor next to him like a floozie." "Why don't you drive on the shoulder like everyone else?"

I would have been reduced to a screaming lunatic, crushing half-full cans of soda in one hand, throwing them out the car window, slamming on the brakes, leaping out of the car, and stomping away.

Psychological warfare, my father called this tactic of hers. She's an expert at it. I take a breath and remind myself that no one is only one thing. I search my memory, looking for one good moment, and find it. She chaperoned my eighth-grade graduation party at my teacher's house when no other parent would. My teacher was a Black man. It was 1959 in Jim Crow America, and she danced with him. My son's right: she's brave.

My son takes my hand to lead me to the dance floor. I briefly lean against him, knowing this is the day I give him permission to leave me. He asks, "Where's Grandma Zuzu?" I tell him what my sister told me. "She's feeling weak." I stroke his face. "But it doesn't matter. This is your day." He grins.

I look around for my husband, who's dancing with our new daughter-in-law. They already adore each other. It's me of whom my sons' wives are wary.

"You can be cruel, Mom," this truth-teller son once said.

I stopped in my tracks, frozen, knowing I hadn't escaped my genes. *There's a dragon in me. If I'm not careful, I'll scorch everything in my path with a flick of my tongue.* Regret weighs as much as shame. I vowed to do better than my mother did. Memories of my failures lurk in my children's minds like hidden code, waiting to be deciphered, uncoiled, and flare unexpectedly.

When the dance ends, and I look up at my son's face, I see love and kindness. We change partners, and I dance with my husband. My face nestles against his shoulder, and I recall taking my mother to meet him, this man who feels like home to me.

We stood in his kitchen just long enough for hello, my way of minimizing the risk she would reduce him to char and smoke. He took our photograph and made jokes, and then I whisked her away for lunch at the local diner—Formica tables, red plastic booth seats, paper placemats emblazoned with ads, fake plants. Not the kind of place she would have taken me. For a while, we chatted amicably, as if we were any mother and daughter.

Then she pushed her dessert aside. "Why did you run away from me?"

I peeled the wrapper from a straw. She'd returned to the refrain of our relationship in which she's the innocent victim, and I'm the agent of her pain. I wondered how her view of us got so skewed. Rolling the paper into a ball between my fingers, I said, "To save myself." *Because you're insane,* I refrained from uttering, still holding back the truth to protect her.

"Is saving yourself more important to you than me?"

I sighed, knowing I shouldn't try to answer her loaded question, knowing no sane mother would ask it. She didn't even know she had the relationship backward and inside out. It was never my job to save her; she wasn't supposed to be my highest priority. She was supposed to protect me.

I wanted to be kind, but I had to stand up for myself, for the child who deserved saving. "Yes," I said, searching for words that would heal her without erasing me. "Saving myself is important."

Her face flushed; her fingers crumpled the paper placemat. She was preparing.

I should have run, but I was older now and thought I could handle this. "Maybe you should ask God for forgiveness."

"I don't believe in God." Her eyes blazed. "There is no God." Spit flew out of her mouth. She slammed her hand on the table. "I want *you* to forgive me."

I stared at her. A kind of terror shook me, and then sorrow, the kind a child feels when she discovers she can't count on the people she loves. I could release her, but I remember her coming into my room at night after she whipped me. She would sit on the side of my bed, pull the hair off my wet cheeks, and say, "I'm sorry. I didn't mean to. I don't know what comes over me. Forgive me."

I would lie and say, "I forgive you," knowing the words didn't matter, knowing she would hit me again. Saying I forgave her was part of my punishment; saying it made me betray myself. She knew this. I always thought she relished that part the most.

I'm done with this cycle. I shook my head and turned my face away. Not now. Not anymore. I stared into her angry, mournful eyes. Maybe not ever.

The music stops, signaling the end of my son's wedding. Everyone gathers on the porch to say goodbye. I feel empty and full, left behind and released. I want to remember everything from today and know I'm already forgetting. I recall my son sitting at the head table with the bride's veil on his head. We toasted them, and everyone applauded.

I hold my breath. We're a family careful with hope. We know we should never be too sure of anything. Still, we stretch out our arms for normal as if that's the gold ring, and when we catch it, we know enough to celebrate. My son kisses my cheek, and I exhale. From the abundance of his happiness, he has forgiven me.

UNMENTIONABLES

My mother tells me she's outwitted the thief who wants to steal her underwear. Three months ago, the doctors said she would die of congestive heart failure in three days. She's outwitted them also. She's worried about her underwear, not dying.

We're in this together. At this moment, when everything counts, we're talking about protecting her underwear. All those pretty garments stashed in a box under her bed are a metaphor for something I don't want to decode.

"No one will think to look there," she says.

Insistent, urgent, specific, and irate. She's angry at the unfairness of everything. It's not bad enough that she grew old, she can no longer keep the wolves from the door, and she's dying—now they're after her underwear. Her eyes, bombs with lit fuses, flare.

She shares her strategy with me, so I'll be her aide-de-camp in her war against the underwear thieves. I wade through the words hoping to find a way to reassure her that no one will take her panties. Uneasiness stirs my stomach. There's history at work here, a more terrifying, unmentionable theft she's never told me. There's a story that might explain everything, a story that, in the end, I don't want to know. Perhaps certain things should not be uncovered. Maybe the truth isn't enough.

All I could say was, "Good plan."

Her hands are cold; her legs are hot. She throws off the sheet. For weeks she's been sleeping almost continually, or what passes for sleep. Periodically she punctuates the long silence by slamming the flat of her hand against the mattress. "Enough!" she yells. "Enough. Enough."

Today she's talking. When I ask about this new phase, the hospice nurse frankly says that she may be talkative today, but it's all part of the dying process. She says this phase is a kind of illumination as the body heals itself before the final sigh. I take this explanation with a grain of salt. I don't believe anyone knows anything about dying.

My mother pauses and daintily puts the tip of her pointer finger against the corner of her mouth. She dabs away the grit that has gathered there out of nowhere. Her nails are cut short but are still painted red at her insistence. Her white hair has been brushed into two short pigtails at the top of her head by the nurse's aide, who intends to be kind but has no sense of irony.

Back to the ninety pounds she swears she was when pregnant with me, she wears an adult diaper and a blazing red t-shirt. Her speech is difficult to understand, and lucid moments are rare. I lean in. We conspire together against what's next.

"The people here don't like me," she says, waving toward the nursing home hallway. "My daughter thinks I don't know this, but I do." Her brown eyes blaze with indignation. Then she smiles her winning smile and asks me to run across the hall to the nurses' station and fetch her chocolate ice cream in a paper cup.

On my way to get the ice cream I know she won't eat, I remember standing in the bedroom I'd given her in my home, my entire body shaking with rage.

"Where did you put the checks?" I ask when I discover she has stolen blank checks from my checkbook.

She lifts her chin and looks out the window at my safe suburban neighborhood. She's in complete control of this situation even though she's old, frail, and living in my house.

In the mirror over her desk, I catch a glimpse of the shock and despair on my face as I ask again, thinking she might not have heard me. She wants to harm me. Her theft brings up every old attack she ever launched against me. I'm a child again, helpless against her, raging.

She shrugs and smirks. "Behind the boy," she says.

The boy? Behind what boy? She's being coy, manipulating me. I struggle to be rational, to think my way through this maze. I'm good at compartmentalizing my feelings and engaging my left brain. I look around the room and see the framed photograph of my sister's son, the boy whose name my mother has forgotten. I pick up the picture, open the back, find the checks folded into a tiny square, and extract them.

"Why did you do this?" I ask her, even though I know she doesn't know why. We're playing out an old drama. She must steal something from me to be even for having endured the agony of having me. I ruined her life, she always said. To be even, she must take every-thing—my identity, my father, my sister, my money.

She stares at me with the look that used to precede a beating. She doesn't have the strength to hit me, but she can still stun. "If I had a gun," she says, "I would kill you."

I walk out of the room, go downstairs, and outside to the porch. I breathe deeply for ten minutes, waiting for the mountains and trees to calm me. Then I go inside, call her doctor, and tell the nurse what she said.

"You know how it is," she says, returning me to the present, her room in the nursing home. I hand her the opened ice cream and a spoon. "The last thing you remember, you were watching *Gone with the Wind* on the movie channel, then suddenly you're standing in the produce section in your pink nightgown as if you'd walked all the way to Tara in a dream."

She pauses again, for effect this time, to see if I've gotten the joke. I nod and smile, appreciating her sense of humor. I take her hand, but she complains that my hand is too hot. I remind myself we're not close. I shouldn't expect anything new.

Being smart, my mother always said, was being able to devise solutions to whatever problem presented itself. I look out of the win-dow, watching the afternoon shadow thrown by the building cross the grassy hill and ride along the fence. Sometimes it's hard to look at her, this dying stranger who doesn't look like my mother. I have no solution for this problem, but that difference allows me to be kind.

She explains her new strategy for dressing. "I just wear a flowered housedress. I'm always presentable when guests arrive. If I find myself in the hallway unexpectedly and don't remember if I've thrown trash down the chute or I'm on my way to the laundry room, I'm still respectable."

I wonder if she threw her underwear down the trash chute instead of putting it in the washing machine. What if the theft of her underwear is about a monster who came in the night and stole her virginity? I don't say anything. Either way, how would it matter now?

She's silent for a while, her eyes closed, breathing slowed. I realize she doesn't know where she is. It's dark in the room. I look at my watch, at the photographs tacked up on the bulletin board hung on the wall at the foot of her bed. My sister put them up to help her recapture her memories. In one of them, a woman with abundant brunette hair strikes a provocative pose with a man I don't know. That is the mother I remember.

When she opens her eyes, I ask who the man in the photo is. She says, "Oh, I don't know. He doesn't matter." Decades dissolve in disinterest. Perhaps she never cared.

Her bed is backward in the room, facing away from her roommate. The footboard is against the wall so she can lie in bed, propped up on pillows, and watch her TV. She's on her fourth roommate since she's been in the nursing home. The others have all died.

Few of my mother's precious things remain from the last thirty years of frenzied collecting. Enamel plaques with stylized stone flowers bought in Hong Kong hang on the wall to the left of her bed. The hand-painted lingerie dresser with scrolled brass drawer pulls stands to the right of the television and holds dozens of pairs of colorful socks rolled into balls. Her upholstered rocker faces the television, away from her roommate. And, of course, the frilly French unmentionables, the underwear she never wears anymore, are in a box under the bed.

A nurse complained to me a month ago that my mother insisted on wearing two pairs of adult diapers simultaneously. She's planning a quick getaway. If the prince pinned to the wall comes to her rescue, she'll be ready to fly the coop, an expression of hers that always made me imagine fluttering wings and a snowstorm of feathers.

"When I lived in Hawaii, we called these dresses muumuus," she says suddenly, picking up the thread of her thought. "Muumuu is the perfect word," she tells me. "You want to murmur something soothing when you're wearing them."

She drifts off, and I sit there, empty, incapable of solving the problem of death.

"Have you told her you forgive her?" the hospice nurse asks when she bustles in for a vitals check.

"As much as I can," I say, and don't even ask how the nurse knows I'm supposed to perform this ritual. We're all priests now, absolving those who trespassed against us so they may go unburdened to heaven.

Is there an invisible tattoo on my forehead that marks my tribe? Those who must forgive. Perhaps it's a pictogram or a spiky hieroglyphic of fear, rage, and sorrow. Maybe the clue is in how far I sit from my mother's bed.

The nurse places her fingers on the inside of my mother's wrist. "Thready," she says as if I know what that portends. "You should tell her it's okay to go."

"Don't let that woman vacuum under the bed," my mother mutters.

I giggle. It's too late now to distress her with questions about her childhood, too late to ferret out the story of the thief who comes in the night and steals her most private things. I turn away from this thought again. I can't bear the effort of hating anyone today.

She tells me she put her best undergarments under the sofa cushions. "When I sleep on the sofa, no one will be able to get them."

"Perfectly logical," I say.

She looks at me with alarm, as if she had forgotten something critical or was suddenly afraid. "Did Willie call?" she asks for the third time in three days.

I shake my head no. Willie died years ago, but I dare not say that. Instead, I tell her I can stay a while longer. I pour water from the pitcher into her glass, place the tip of my finger over the top of the straw and watch the water being sucked upward by the vacuum into the straw. I hold the straw near her lips, slowly dripping water into her mouth.

She sips, licks her lips, and turns her face away. "That's enough," she says, not having eaten for three weeks. She asks if I'm hungry and offers to ring for ice cream.

I shake my head no. "I don't need anything. Tell me about the muumuus."

"Never be unkempt in front of strangers," she declares. "It was the Depression. I was the ninth child. My mother could have cared less about what happened to me. She never had time for me. I just tagged along behind Willie."

This is her refrain. I've heard it all my life. I've never known what to do with the information. When I was a child, she used to tell me my clothes were clean and paid for. It was a point of pride, something to use as a rebuttal when attacked. We expected to be attacked. We had contingency plans. I realize now she gave me a weapon she didn't have when she was young: clean clothes.

I offer her water again, putting the straw to her mouth. It dribbles down her chin. I blot her mouth with a white tissue. "Oh, excuse me, my mouth just isn't where it should be," she says. "Something always falls out."

It's an old joke. I smile. We are people who spill things. Our minds are always somewhere else.

"They're killing people here," she says. "Strange things happen. I've tried to tell my daughter about them, but she just says, 'Oh, Mom, I'm sure that's not true.' My daughter thinks she can talk me out of believing what I know."

I nod slightly. She's right. I used to think I could talk her out of her paranoia. I've reformed. Paranoia is what happens to you when you're haunted by evil as a child, taken by it, violated at will. The past makes you vigilant. There are signs of imminent danger everywhere. I see what she sees. People are dying. The effective plan here is to escape.

"There was that fire when we all had to be evacuated," she reminds me.

That wasn't in the nursing home. She's flipped to four years ago, remembering the apartment where she lived for years before she came to stay with me. Time, distance, and space are irrelevant. In a blink, memory sets one thing against another, rearranging the narrative's atoms, and changing its species and genus. Years ago, her apartment building was evacuated in the middle of the night because of a fire that started in her kitchen. I wonder if all memories are like this—a kernel of fact around which nacreous layers of invention are secreted.

She returns to her underwear, the recurring melody of her old age. She tells me I need to be wary of the woman who comes to clean because she'll want to vacuum under the bed.

"My daughter is in cahoots with the cleaning woman," she says. "She can't wait to get her hands on my things."

She's quiet again for a while, her eyes closed. Her breathing is what the nurse calls shallow. Her arm is icy cold when I touch it. I pull the cover over her legs. My mind wanders. I think about what I'll prepare for dinner and make a shopping list in my head.

"You need to be careful about telling your daughter everything," she says in the barest whisper.

I startle.

"I can tell you that daughters come and go around here. You can hear them walking the hallway if you lower the sound on the television. They walk up and down the hallway as if they were waiting for someone to give birth. I'm sure you know about giving birth."

She gives me the once over, able to tell by looking at me whether I've succeeded in that department. I've given up reminding her she has grandsons. Perhaps she remembers for a minute; then, another memory whisks her away.

All of a sudden, her face turns toward the hallway. She asks, "Is Willie coming?"

I surrender and nod, consoling her, "He's on his way."

I stroke her arm. She drifts off for a bit or does what passes for sleep. The cells of her body stray into the air around her. I think about who she is, her obstinacy, her determination to save the last shreds of her dignity.

"It's okay to go, Mom, if you want to."

The nurse comes in for rounds and another semblance of taking her patient's vitals. They're charting the countdown, the soul's liftoff into the ether. I'm inured to this. I gather my things to go, and my mother wakes abruptly, turns her head, and looks at me in panic, wordless, her eyes wide with terror, her mouth open without a sound.

"I'll be back," I say from the door. "Don't worry." I still haven't said I forgive her. I'm working up to it, debating with myself about the utility of forgiveness. Is it a blessing she takes with her, a coin she can use to gain heaven? The words hang heavy in my chest like an obligation, but I'm not ready.

I wave goodbye from the door. Holding my breath, I walk quickly through the halls to the back door on the lower level. I punch in the code to release the door lock. All my focus is on escape. Outside, I exhale and take deep breaths of the cold March air. I open all the windows in the car and leave them open the entire drive home to shed the smell of impending death.

Four hours later, the nurse calls. "She's gone," she says, her voice quivering.

My mother has flown the coop, and all that's left are white feathers in a box under the bed.

FINDING BARGAINS AT THE COSMIC FIVE AND DIME

My sister, standing behind the oak pulpit in the chapel, readies herself to speak. She presses her lips together, her blue eyes calm in an ever-pale face. We settle into our seats. She has always known how to command. She waits for quiet—one beat, two. Then it's quiet as death in the sanctuary.

Behind her, the Torah is safely stowed in its sleek oak case, untouched by grief. Blue and white lights stream from stained glass windows and braid themselves together across the floor. Death needs only a simple ceremony, an acknowledgment that God always wins. I sit in the front row with my husband and son, waiting my turn to speak.

We recite a prayer, reading from the program in our hands, to honor the space, not our mother, who was not a member of this congregation. I recall sitting with her in a crowded restaurant with the sound of clinking flatware and casual conversations buzzing around us. My suggestion then that she ask God for forgiveness was as incendiary as if I'd held her bare hand to the fire. I expected her to spit and throw salt over her shoulder.

Her brown eyes boring into me, she had demanded my forgiveness. I should have asked, "For what?" and made her say the words, name the crimes, admit her complicity, but I learned long ago that words abandon me when I most need them, that holding back tears stifles all sound. I couldn't touch her hand or say the words she desired. Withholding forgiveness—the one thing she ever wanted from me—was the only power I had.

She died without it.

My sister describes our mother's life, her vibrancy. I recall what she doesn't say. I picture our mother dancing in the kitchen, her arms whirling, feet tapping. "Flat foot floozy with a floy floy," she sang, the meaningless words matching her sizzling energy. I see her striding toward me down a hospital corridor, her scarf streaming behind her, her face painted with a brilliant red smile. She wasn't sick. She had just wanted to audition new doctors. I look down at the paper in my hand and silently re-read the piece my sister assigned me.

My grief is a dry well.

"What would be the point in weeping?" I'd asked my husband, who stood next to me after the nurse told me my mother was dead. He was wordless; hands held out to embrace me if I wanted, head tilted, trying to understand. Memories ping off the walls of the well on the way to the bottom, like a penny thrown in for good luck, for wishes that will never come true.

Sarah tells the assembled that our mother was dauntless. It's not a word I would choose. I look down at the text in my hand and re-read the first line: "Do not stand at my grave and weep. I am not there." I wonder why my sister chose this piece for me to read. My mind drifts back fifteen years.

After the fact, my mother told me about her heart attack. I imagined her arteries narrowing, plaque ripping from the arterial wall, and blocking blood flow to the heart. Her neck hurt, she said. When she vomited, she blamed the Halloween party food at her active senior neighborhood clubhouse. She was dizzy. Pain sliced through her chest like lightning. Her face was cold, but she was sweating. She sat on the edge of the tub. Her jaw hurt. She knew something was wrong and phoned for an ambulance. As she described her experience, I wondered if she'd been wearing her witch costume, complete with the black sequined hat.

The day before the triple bypass surgery, my mother said she was donating her body to science so we wouldn't have to bury her. "In case anything happens, I'm ready to die if it's my time." Husband number five, the last, had already died. She lived alone. She sounded matter of fact. "I've made my peace," she said.

The breath went out of me. I'd never expected her to be mortal. She was seventy-eight. My indomitable archenemy, defiant in the face of everything, couldn't die. Who would I struggle against if she died? Who would I be?

As we waited to see what happened after her open-heart surgery, my son reminded me that she was brave. He gave me the look that meant I was supposed to be kind. Kindness was a shiny bauble on a high shelf in a shop that sold nothing I could afford.

My sister's eulogy drones on in the background. *Irresponsible is a better word for her. No, incorrigible.* Hackles up, I'm on my guard against the fear that I've lost what I never had.

Before her surgery, my mother told me about accounts she had in four banks, both hers and her sister Mellie's, for whom she had power of attorney. My head reeled. She knew the numbers cold. She told me the names of the banks and the amounts that had to be moved from one account to another to write checks.

"Are you writing this down?" she asked.

I laughed and flashed on her dexterity with money when we lived on twenty-five dollars a week in the Seth Boyden housing project in Newark, New Jersey. We were never hungry. We always had clothes and shoes and a place to sleep. My perspective tilted as if I had been looking too closely at something, and when I looked again, the picture was completely different. For a moment, I saw the world from her point of view, that at any second, everything might fall apart, and we'd have to live on the street, cast out with no food, no clothes, shivering, sleeping in alleys, jumping at every noise in the dark. Desperate without options. No wonder she tried to escape. No wonder she danced in the kitchen and wished for a prince. And then the image was gone.

After the surgery, she didn't have the strength to talk. The next day, still heavily sedated, she could speak for five minutes. I imagined her zooming along the freeways of California at eighty miles an hour, talking police officers out of tickets, zipping into trinket and second-hand shops where she made the owner's entire season with purchases of a dozen *tchotchkes*. She would suffocate without her wild freedom.

We laid out the future in small steps that we could accomplish. She complained of feeling claustrophobic. My sister sorted her dozens of pills into small containers. I wanted to run away.

"Soon, she'll be dancing in the streets," the doctor assured us.

We didn't believe him.

Two years beyond the surgery, she called at midnight, 9 P.M. on her side of the continent. By now, her white hair floated up from her head, defying gravity. She held it down with a wig. With one good eye and barely five feet tall, she used a cane to walk and still drove on California freeways alone. Independence was her mantra.

She was just getting home, she said. Her fury flashed across the phone line. She had to tell someone about this day, down to the smallest detail. She'd been visiting her sister in a hospital sixty miles away and spent the day fighting with nurses to get attention for her. "Simple things," she said, "like clean her up, make sure she eats something, and make her comfortable."

When staff paid no attention, she planted her feet in the middle of the hallway and called for a nurse until someone came. "Nurse, nurse, nurse, nurse, I need help here, nurse," she shrieked like a young child demanding food. I remembered Uncle Willie's story, how he willed himself into catatonia to get his way.

I wondered if something was wrong with us, with our fierce determination to get what we wanted at all costs. We focus; we never give up. Then I remember these are the genes that get you over the Alps in winter, wearing a cloth coat with a baby strapped to your back.

After six hours of caring for her sister, my mother drove her twelve-year-old, twenty-six-foot-long 1985 baby blue Oldsmobile into a gas station to top off for the ride home. "All I wanted was to get home before dark," she explained. "I can't see at night." Her indignation twanged across three thousand miles.

She signaled to two young men lounging against a fence at the gas station and held up her disability card. "Gas station attendants in California are supposed to help the old and infirm at self-help pumps," she explained.

A thin young man with long blond hair, wearing jeans low on his hips, walked over to her car window and asked what she needed. "You know the type," she said, "a hoodlum." "Gas," she reminded me, "is a dollar and nineteen cents a gallon." He took the fifteen dollars she handed him and went inside the office.

The young man came out of the office, pumped thirteen dollars and thirty-nine cents worth of gas into her car, and said to her, "It's full."

She put her hand outside her window and asked for her change. "There's no change," he said.

"There should be a dollar-sixty-one in change," she retorted.

"Nope," he said, "I bought a pack of cigarettes as my tip."

"That's not your tip. I decide if you get a tip. I want my change."

"No way." He batted his hand at her and walked away.

She leaned out the window and yelled after him, "You're a crook!"

He looked over his shoulder. "And your teeth are falling out of your head."

She took her keys, got out of the car, hobbled on her cane into the office, and demanded her change. The cashier, chewing gum and smoking a cigarette, denied all knowledge of the transaction. "That guy's not a gas station employee," the woman told her, shrugging her shoulders in indifference.

"Call the police," my mother demanded. "He stole my money."

The cashier said she wouldn't. My mother said she wasn't leaving until she got her change. Meanwhile, her car was parked blocking two gas pumps, she told me, glee sparkling around the edges of her fury.

A line of cars formed; a crowd gathered. Other customers came into the office and tried to talk sense into her. "What's a dollar-sixty-one?" they chided. They looked at her and said, "Why risk a heart attack fighting with this kid?"

"Let the guy have his cigarettes as a tip," the cashier said. She slipped her hand under her shirt to adjust her bra strap. "He helped you, and he didn't have to."

My mother didn't budge. "He cheated me," she said, staring at each person, one by one, right in the eyes.

The guy who pumped her gas said, "Get out of here, you old Jew."

She stood leaning on her cane and fixed him with a glare. "You Nazi criminal."

The crowd gasped.

Before the long scar on her chest, my mother would have decked this guy with her cane. Even old, she was capable of sudden violence. Once, she told me with pride, she knocked her neighbor to the ground and sat on her after the woman uprooted the flowers in the bed between their driveways.

"I put the flowers there with my own hands," she said, in her mind totally justified.

Both husbands had stood by, mortified, helpless, while their seventy-year-old wives scratched and clawed. The police came and threatened arrest if my mother didn't get up.

"Taught her a lesson," she said, righteous anger caught in her teeth. "She never did that again." My mother was fierce. She tolerated no assaults on her territory. I realized that I liked this about her.

Finally, a stranger at the gas station handed her two dollars and said, "Here's your change. You should leave now, and you better not come back to this station."

"I'll be back," she said, sounding like a distant cousin of the Austrian-born California governor, and drove off. Well after dark by then, she navigated her way home by instinct rather than sight.

Her rage dissipated as she told me the story.

I asked, "Is a dollar-sixty-one worth dying for?"

She sighed as if to say I would never understand. "It's the principle of the thing. . . ."

My nephew takes his turn at the podium. He's not happy standing there. My sister's done a good job with him. Even when he's miserable, he has poise.

That was one of my mother's words, a word that never had anything to do with our lives. The world conspired with her, letting her skip through disasters without noticing that lives were at stake. She lived in a dream.

She never complained about California's earthquakes and mud-slides or its thousands-of-acres wildfires. After a 7.2 earthquake along the San Andreas Fault, she called to assure me she did not drown. The reservoir in the hills above her town didn't spill its contents. Temecula, east of the Santa Rosa Mountains, where she lived for twenty years, is practically desert but has good soil for grapes and avocados. Here, the native Pechangas believe, is the place of the sun where life began on earth; it's the place of the union of Sky-father and Earthmother. My mother sat on her front porch every morning, drank her coffee, and read the paper.

"I feel like a queen," she told me.

The natural disasters that mattered, the events that set the earth shaking, were what happened to her siblings. Teddy had Alzhei-mer's, Ellie had shingles, Mellie was confined to a wheelchair, and they hoisted her naked body into the bath with a crane. In every call, she listed those who'd died as if she'd just read it in the paper. She still hoped her front door would open and Willie would walk in with apple strudel and tales of the wild life he led in New York City.

I offered nothing but silence on these calls. It was safer that way. Any conversation could leap into flames at the strike of the wrong word against the flint of memory. But how she held onto life taught me we had one chance, and we'd better make the most of it.

My mother's joy was combing through a store filled with other people's bright, shiny, discarded things, determined to find hidden treasure. Her quest was the bargain, the twenty-five-dollar item for fifty cents, the Hockney sketch for a dollar. "If I can't shop, there's no point living," she said.

"What about your grandchildren?" I asked, holding my hand against my chest to hide my anger. The first time she said this, I thought of my grandmother and how my children would never have that deep connection with her, a memory forever sweet.

She looked at me blankly as if I'd asked her to compare diamonds to cotton stockings and shook her head. "You can't understand. Everything came to you so easily." For her, a bargain was the cherry on top of the sundae, the extra taste of something sweet, a way of besting life at its own game.

After she moved, her two-bedroom apartment within walking distance from my sister's was packed with stuff she didn't need. She filled every inch of space with treasures that made up for a childhood with nothing. Glass-door cabinets displayed tiny China teacups hand painted with pink roses and ruby-colored lead-glass vases heaped with multi-colored pop-it beads. She had metal statues of naked, voluptuous women made into lamps she must have gotten from a brothel liquidation. Celadon and malachite necklaces, jasper, and silver bracelets filled desk drawers.

In her eighties, driver's license gone, she made it to her favorite haunts by hitching rides with sympathetic strangers or trawling for rides in the lobby of her building when neighbors were going out with family, snaring them in a net of sympathy. Sometimes she stood in the parking lot and asked if someone was going to the market, or walked out into the street, leaned over her walker, and held out her thumb to hitch.

My eyes rolled. How do you tell an eighty-five-year-old woman who survived the Depression, life in the projects, and five husbands that she can't ask people to give her a lift?

"So what's the worst they could do?" She chuckled. "Kill me?"

I remember standing with her on Frelinghuysen Avenue in Newark, the factory behind us, her gloved hand in the air, her skirt billowing, waving down an accommodating motorist. Eight years old, I tugged on her sleeve, anxious. "Mommy, we can wait for the bus."

She pulled her arm away, leaned over, and smiled at the man who slowed his car. She opened the door, and we piled in. She chattered to him, and I glowered at her from the back seat, sure she would get us all killed.

We went to a movie, sitting through it twice, plus the cartoon and the coming attractions. On the bus fare we saved, after the movie, we went to the diner where they served complete meals for a dollar—liver and onions, mashed potatoes, string beans, applesauce.

Somehow, she got our meals for free. I relished my rye bread with butter. She held my sister's hand, and we walked home from there.

She dressed us up—me in lime green, Sarah in blue—and took us to lunch in the Rainbow Room at the top of the Rockefeller Center building. Twice we had lunch in the posh garden restaurant in Central Park. Where did she find the money? We walked to the beach through Honolulu's Royal Hawaiian Hotel lobby, and she held her head up like a queen. I waited, rigid with fear, expecting to be told we didn't belong, that we had to leave.

Sitting at her funeral, waiting to speak, I smile at her antics and think she had some nerve. It's my turn to read. I go to the podium and face the people who came to help us mourn. My husband and son smile at me. I read the first line out loud and then the second, "I do not sleep." At the third, my voice falters, "I am a thousand winds that blow." I lose it by the middle of the poem, all the anguish held inside rushing into sound, all the things we didn't say, all the times I walked away from her now leaving me as tears.

I grip the wooden pulpit, look at my sister, and say, "Thanks a lot."

She grimaces.

Returning to the text, I take deep breaths and stumble through the lines, determined, like my mother, to hold my head up to make it to the end. "Do not stand at my grave and cry," I read. "I am not there. I did not die."

In a flash, I'm a child standing in Macy's at Christmastime surrounded by acres of glittering things, and suddenly I understand what she's given me. For the rest of my life, I have all these memories, and all they cost were a few moments of time.

THE PHYSICS OF THINGS

My husband sits in his chair in the family room, a coffee cup on the table beside him. He no longer reads or even wants to read, but the laptop is open on the coffee table in case one of the kids wants to chat. His eyes light up when the computer pings.

Standing at the back door, looking out at our backyard, I inhale deeply. "It smells so good out there. I'm going to cut flowers."

He nods. "Go ahead. I'm okay."

Fifty feet from the house, huge hydrangea bushes, branches heavy with cones of white flowers, dip their heads toward the ground. I don't take my phone. I won't be gone long. Twenty minutes later, I enter the kitchen, my arms loaded with freshly cut flowers—long stems of white hydrangeas with octave-wide green leaves, sprigs of lavender, stalks of pink Echinacea, and stems of blue Russian sage, each tiny, curled petal its own miracle.

"Look what I've got," I say.

He's leaning back in the chair, mouth stretched open as if he had been gulping air, drowning, or screaming for me. I touch his chest, his face: no sound, no breath, no pulse. I lean against the sofa, and when sound comes, it comes howling, wordless.

I stutter through the hospice call. The room is full of death. *Death is contagious*, an ancient part of me thinks, *an obscenity that offends my sense of propriety*. I call my sons and pace the house.

I pretend the sweet fragrance of flowers mingled with the smell of freshly brewed coffee was his last experience, that he took an aromatic reminder of home, a ghostly tag of the living into the next realm. It's not too far a reach. He believes in heaven.

We once discussed corporeality after death. Of course, we disagreed. I'm lying to myself, hoping something of the life he knew with me went with him like the aroma of a memory to the great hereafter. In his vision of heaven, he's still himself, standing in the reeds at the edge of a rushing creek and fishing. I imagine him there, smell the deep green decay of the water, see flies circling above the stream, and hear leaves rustle. He smiles at me.

The night we met, he stood against a bar rail in a dusky hotel ballroom at a singles dance. He wore a beard and a light blue polo shirt that matched his eyes. Brown hair curled across his forehead and down his neck. My pupils widened, my breath hastened, and my cheeks flushed.

I asked, "Do you dance?"

"Yes, I do." He put down his beer and tamped out his cigarette.

He took me in his arms and sang softly in my ear, his breath on my cheek. No one ever fell faster than I did. A week later, he came to my house, looked at my books, walked into my kitchen, and marked up my typed, three-column list of the perfect man's attributes I had taped to the refrigerator door to remind me who I was searching for.

"Sense of humor," he added in perfect engineer's block print, a joke I get now, decades later. He can still make me laugh.

I sit in the kitchen and call my sister and stepsister. Although he didn't die in bed, I change the bed and run a wash of sheets and towels. I attack the refrigerator with steaming hot water and soap, scrubbing off sticky juices accumulated on glass shelves, scouring out death.

Shudders take me. I have to do something else. I look around the kitchen and take all the knives out of the wooden knife block, washing them in the sink with steaming hot water and detergent. I dry them, place them in descending order by size on the counter and clean the block that held them until the bamboo gleams. Sorting knives is the sole action I can control.

I attempt more order, emptying the junk drawer and arranging implements by size—long-handled salad spoons and a cheese grater, can openers with the nutcracker, scissors, garlic press, bottle opener, corn-on-the-cob holders—and lay them across the counter like surgical instruments. I scrub the drawer and dry it.

My body reboots as if someone else pushed a button. When I look up from organizing the junk drawer, he's still in his chair. His head—hair cropped in what we, laughing away our agony, called his Marine cut when he could no longer raise his arms to brush it—leans forward just a bit.

I hold in a sob and go into my office to email friends. I post his death on social media and call the funeral home, the one he chose a year ago. Scrambling through emails to me, I find the obituary he wrote. It needs editing. I leave it open on the screen.

What would I have said if I'd been sitting next to him? Goodbye, I guess. I could have said goodbye if I had been able to speak.

I imagine his last words. "Honey, where the hell are you?"

❋

"He suffocated," the hospice doctor says after she confirms his death. She signs forms. "Someone on the team will do what they're supposed to about removing the body."

The body. I can't grasp this concept; I won't. I blame myself for this death. I forgot everything I was supposed to do, everything I read and know.

The doctor reads my face. "The answer has to do with his illness," she attempts to comfort me, "how his lungs turned to stone. There was nothing you could do."

After she leaves, I notice flowers strewn on the floor, the chair near the door, and the table. I forgot I dropped them. I walk around them for a while, as if picking them up and putting them in water is a betrayal. Then I gather them up, pinching each stalk as if it's the enemy, keeping each at arm's length, and throw them in the kitchen trash bin, thinking of the last couple of days.

❋

"What are you going to do with my wedding ring?" he asked two evenings before he died. The television is on, but the sound is muted.

139

He claims movies are better this way because he can make up his own dialogue.

I'm washing dishes and turn off the water to hear him better. "I'm going to wear it."

He's quiet for a while as if this answer needs to percolate through a filter. "Will you get married again?"

I'm ready for this question, having thought about it. "No, you're enough. This is enough. I don't want anyone after you."

He closes his eyes and leans his head back against the soft, red corduroy pillow, a small comfort I gave him against the long ache of dying from a terminal illness.

"I'll probably keep talking to you," I say.

"I know you will."

I hear his smile rather than see it. "Do you think you'll hear me?"

He says nothing.

I dry my hands and walk to where he can see me. "If you do talk to me, I'll probably jump out of my skin. At first, anyway. You'll have to find a way to let me know beforehand."

He nods and smiles that grim smile I know so well. "I was really bad about your mother," he says.

In her last months, he went with me twice to the nursing home, sitting stony-faced and unforgiving, unspeaking, looking anywhere but at her. He was my white knight defending me against my last dragon when what I needed, what we all needed, was compassion.

I go back to putting dishes in the machine. "Yes, you were."

"I didn't know what she was going through. I get it now."

I don't answer. It would take another lifetime to answer.

I pull myself together and stop performing futile tasks. Waiting for the funeral home staff to remove him, I sit in my chair, close enough to lean over and touch his hand. It's still warm. I hold it loosely as if gripping it would hurt or disturb him.

"I love you," I say, just in case he can still hear me.

I want to climb into his lap and burrow my face in his neck. I want his arms around me. I have no understanding of how death works. Is there a part of him that's still here with me? I want to go back to the beginning and start again.

A month ago, gaunt, jaundiced, eyes burning, he turned his face to me and said, "You're so beautiful."

I was playing solitaire. That look in his eyes was all the love I ever wanted. No one ever looked at me the way he did. "I love you, too, you know," I said, ducking my head, terrified.

"I always wait too long," he murmured.

Then a week before he died, he opened his eyes and whispered, "I just had the most wonderful conversation with you."

I was bringing in groceries from the car. Speechless, I stopped moving, breath held, watching light swirl around his head. I saw him riding a boogie board through the boiling surf, rolling right up to my ankles. Sunlight glinted off his wet, tan shoulders. He shook the hair out of his eyes and grinned. I exhaled, helplessly swept up in his joy, and grinned back at him.

On Rome's Palatine Hill, surrounded by sun-kissed marble debris, he breathed in deeply, a blissful smile on his upturned lips; his eyes gleamed. Standing in front of Bernini's sculptures, he sighed, swept away by beauty and surprise.

We held hands and stepped into the turquoise silk of the clear Pacific where living sea anemones and sand dollars moved on white sand between black volcanic rocks off a Tofino beach. We were careful where we put our feet.

I didn't ask him what we said in his half-dream conversation. I didn't want to deal with last-minute confessions or have to forgive the unforgivable. Now it's too late, now that I've waited too long, I say to him, "I'm glad I married you, just in case you didn't know."

I watch for movement. Perhaps he's not really dead; the doctor could be wrong. I look closer; his lips are blue. His hand is cooling. There's no coming back from this.

"I love you," I say again, hoping hearing is the last thing to go.

I watch as the undertakers zip him into a black plastic bag and take him away.

The first time he held me in his arms, we were dancing, and the palm of his hand moved on my ribcage, one finger brushing the edge of my breast. I breathed into him, our molecules blending in a perfume of musk and cigarettes and sweat.

Now, each independent breath extracts me from him, molecule by molecule, until I'm alone in the room with only a trace of him and the aroma of the white hydrangeas.

That night, I plug in his cell phone, out of habit or because I want to keep something of his working, something he touched every day, kept in his shirt pocket, held in his hands. Then I forget about the phone.

Going through things in the rattan chest in the kitchen, I find his car phone charger. I throw it away, telling myself he won't need it anymore. I throw out inhalers, nebulizers, breath meters, oxygen tubing—all the paraphernalia of his illness. My hands shake.

I trash things I hope I won't need later. I throw my own clothes and shoes into large dark green garbage bags. I toss years of hand-written poems and rip up letters. Throwing things out is my way of getting even with the universe. I delude myself into thinking that if bags of our clothes and shoes go out the door together, somehow, we're still a couple.

I wake up the next morning and realize I'm no longer part of a "we."

One month after his death, the sky is a clear blue dome. Birds call to each other, and a rooster crows in the distance. The house creaks a bit. Smells of autumn fill the air when I step onto the porch to watch the world. Any minute now, I expect him to call out to me, "What are you doing out there?"

"Just breathing, babe," I say out loud. "Just being here."

Now standing at the kitchen sink, watching through the window the impossible slow bloom of a sunlight-yellow magnolia flower in September, it comes to mind, fast, like a door opening on a bright morning from a dark room: *it's all an illusion.*

The thought has nothing to do with what I'm doing. It's unbidden but so urgent and loud in my ears, I ask, "Is that you, honey? Did you say that?"

Only he ever said such things to me.

If it's all an illusion, then he's not dead or any deader than I am. Neither of us is real. Death is not real. Do I get to have him back now? My mind is racing; my eyes dart about the room. I've read the grieving steps. I know I'm bargaining.

If it's all an illusion, will I walk into the family room and see him standing there? Will he ask me, annoyed, "What did you do with my chair?"

"I threw it out," I say to an empty room.

He gives me his annoyed look, lips drawn down, one eyebrow raised, and asks me to fix him a bowl of vanilla ice cream with chocolate syrup as compensation for the missing chair.

"Never mind the ice cream," I say. "We should run away to New Zealand right away. Pack nothing. Take the passports and all the bank cards and go. Go quickly before anyone notices. Before anyone says, 'He's gone. You can't do that.'"

I close my eyes to the still, dark family room.

Oh, to wake up in the morning with him next to me, a sea breeze billowing the sheer curtains, the swish and hiss of sea kissing the sand, and see his chest rise and fall, rise and fall.

I place my hand on his chest. There's a heartbeat. He opens his blue, blue eyes and looks at me. Outside, in the distance, there's a snowcapped mountain. We're free. We.

It's all an illusion.

The house creaks. My husband seems to be walking around upstairs. I hold my breath. He once explained how materials expand in the heat and shrink in the cold.

"But that," I said, "accounts only for the sounds after the heat or the air conditioning come on or abrupt changes in weather."

"The house settles," he said, something about atoms in constant motion, how the earth under us shifts.

It's an explanation I take on faith. But what about the louder banging under the porch every night beginning at eight? What about the painting that flies off the wall in his office so violently that it loses its frame? No one has an answer for me. He's the one who understood the physics of things.

I skip over science and abandon math. The calendar makes no sense. I'm worried I'll lose track or forget when he died, forget when his chest stopped moving, when suddenly there was nothing. I worry my forgetting will be his real death, and I'll tumble through timeless space without anything to stop me.

At the beginning of the third month—all chronological references now reframed into before his death and after—I unplug his phone. It buzzes in my hand. Stunned, I open it. The caller's name on the screen is his. I press the green icon.

"Hello?"

"I need to tell you I love you," he says.

But I dreamed that.

We go to the beach for Thanksgiving, away from home and the traditions we know, but to a place we love. We have no idea how moving our holiday to a strange place will be. Everyone has their trepidations. We're still raw.

On Thanksgiving morning, a cardinal perches in a bush next to the window in the kitchen and watches us. My daughter-in-law takes his photograph. Everyone cooks something. We have our usual feast with a dozen people at the table. We each remember him, a grandson going first. My daughters-in-law sob in each other's arms in the kitchen.

We offer his ashes to the ocean he loved. I'm afraid I won't be able to put my foot on the sand without anguish vanquishing me. But I do. We walk across the sand and stand at the ocean's edge. The day is overcast, the sea is the color of wash water, but calm, and the great rush of sound, wind, and waves are as familiar as a lullaby. I'm home here where he loved to be.

I needn't worry about the ocean. It's big enough, beautiful enough to hold my grief and joy, my memories of him and my sorrow. Still, it's difficult to throw his ashes into the sea, letting go of the physical part of him. Even at the last minute, when I'm trying to set a good example for the kids, I hesitate. He was so much to me; to let him go like that, so thoroughly with nothing held back, is terrifying. My hands fail me. Without speaking, my stepson helps me open the urn.

Our brave boys, grandchildren, daughters, and nephew walk into the water to scatter the gray ash that is all that remains. My youngest son, afraid of the ocean all these years, wades in and ensures every last carbon molecule enters the sea. When we finish, my husband's favorite grandson stands by the shore alone and weeps.

And somehow, my husband is still with me, even in places I've never been.

We see a notice for a community sing scheduled in the old Coast Guard rescue building and walk there. The space is wreathed in garlands. Christmas carols stick in my throat. Music, in general, is impossible, bypassing reason and going straight to the heart. I'm careful with my doses of familiar melodies, but I sing out between gasps, closing my eyes because I can't close my ears.

I hear him singing, his mellow voice caressing my ear. I remember how he was before he was sick when he was the golden angel I found one night by complete accident and got to take home to keep.

TRUE LOVE

My grandson arrived in the world three days before my husband died. After waiting a lifetime for this child, I wanted trumpets and carpets of roses for his entrance, huzzahs and cheering, a Lion King moment. I expected to hear the rush of wings. A host of angels wouldn't be too much.

In the cab on the way to the hospital, I spotted a man striding down Second Avenue in an expensive suit, his red silk tie flying back over his shoulder, a bouquet clutched in one hand, his phone in the other. The sun was shining; he was glowing, and he threw back his head, singing at the sky. I sang with him, racing to meet the love of my life; the world was full of glorious possibilities.

I had planned to whisper to the baby how long I'd waited for him, how beautiful he was, how much he was loved before we ever met—the son of my son, the future of my line, an ordinary mortal's only real immortality. I'd rehearsed my welcoming speech as the train jolted over hundreds of miles of track, and I whispered the words out loud like a mantra to ensure that nothing would go wrong.

Despite my preparation and years of longing and hope, when my son placed that small, warm bundle in my arms, the unexpected fact of him stunned me to silence as every cell in my body transformed, and words were rendered insufficient.

Since the very beginning of humankind, something in the genes waits until grandparenthood to express itself in all its extravagant, heart-blowing glory. Here in that tiny form was the joy we hope to find in life and often don't—a reason for being, the answer to why humanity exists, what we're meant to do.

This tiny being brought everything into focus. My life had not been random at all. Every crazy decision, every lunatic act, every careful choice had all been rushing me headlong toward this moment when I could swallow the sun, and light would leak out of my pores. God exists, I thought and looked at my son—exhausted, exhilarated, terrified, and grinning from ear to ear—and I remembered I felt this way the day *he* was born.

Hours later, at lunch, my other daughter-in-law called me. I could barely make out what she was saying in the din of the packed deli. Pressing the phone to my ear, I asked her to say it again.

"Dad's not going to make it," she said. "His fingernails are turning blue."

On the Formica table in front of me sat the three-inch-high rare roast beef sandwich on real rye bread I'd ordered, the dill pickles and coleslaw, tastes I'd been craving during the last years of my husband's illness. I couldn't imagine eating it. My son's in-laws went on celebrating their grandchild, how beautiful he was, how extraordinary, how amazing.

When I'd said goodbye to my husband the day before, I told him not to leave before I got back. He knew what I meant. The way he looked at me—the light beaming from his blue eyes made my breath stop in my throat. He promised to wait. I thought I had five days, time enough to get my son, his wife, and the baby home and settled before I had to return. I was wrong.

I promised my daughter-in-law I'd come home the next day.

We did our logistics planning: departure times, ticket exchange, the four-hour train ride, and the additional hour-and-a-half drive from the station. Anything could happen in that time. Under strict "no drama" orders from my husband, we didn't weep. No one whined. My companions in the city barely noticed what was going on.

I held my grandson another time, thinking he would never sleep in his grandfather's arms, never be given a nickname. He would never make towers of Legos with his grandfather or ride like a prince on his shoulder. They would never go fishing together, jump in the waves at the beach, or leap into the pool on the count of three. Frisbee, football, basketball—all the nevers leaped to confront me.

Every mile on the train stretched me tauter between the poles of joy and grief.

That night, as the family gathered, my son called using FaceTime and introduced his son to his grandfather on the screen. My husband held the phone and talked to the baby, calling him by name, and the infant considered his grandpa with that grave, piercing baby stare for a full five minutes before they both tired and closed their eyes.

The next morning, my heavily medicated husband asked, "Did the baby come here, or did I go there?"

I explained that they'd met on the phone and that he'd talked to the baby.

"Strange," he said. "I could swear they were here. Are you sure?"

He was quiet, his eyes closed, and then he said, "I just had the most amazing experience. We were fishing, and Augie was in the boat with me. We sat next to each other on the seat, and I put my hand on his knee. I could feel him right there with me."

Like baptism, the naming ceremony, and the first fishing expedition with grandpa.

It was pouring rain on the day my children drove five hours from New York in a ten-year-old Subaru to bring the baby to visit me six weeks after the funeral. All the illness paraphernalia had been removed, and the house cleaned, but there was no way to sweep away death.

The baby had already grown, and I was sure those eyes staring at me were blue. Standing in the family room, rocking, and crooning to our favorite "God Only Knows" song playing in the background, my heart broke open, one half yielding to grief and the other to love beyond anything I'd ever known. My first-born son put his arms around us, and we swayed together, the baby snug against my chest.

Six and a half years later, my grandson, in his first in-person pandemic visit, asks me, "Grandma, what is true love?"

In these two days, he has already asked me more questions than I ever asked my grandmother. We've discussed the nature of the universe and the possibility of time travel. We wrote a story together, August sitting on the couch in my office, writing in his notebook, telling me who the characters are, including the grandmother who believes in all the stories. His story, dictated to me so I could type it, began with, "It was a time of great peril."

There wasn't a moment to lose in our conversation about love. Without blinking, I say, "Kiss me right here on my cheek."

He leans over and presses his lips against my skin.

"You are my true love," I say.

His head tilts as he considers this for a moment, and then he goes on to whatever's next in his busy day. And in an instant, I realize that all I was ever supposed to do with my one life was simply to love him.

HIS STORY

Y ou write my story," my stepson said. "I want you to."

It was a recurrent request I always declined for many rea
sons, but mostly to unsettle his egotism. I wasn't an innocent in our
conflict, even when he stood nose to nose with me, his hands curled
into fists, eyes boring into mine, the threat implicit. Someone had to
stand up to him.

He called once a year to say he was coming for a visit. We would
set a date, but he would never show. It was safer that way.

"Write your own story. That's your job," I said. I thought the task
would give him a purpose. God knows he needed one.

He got eight pages into the story—as far as he ever got no matter
how often he started—his very flawed protagonist waking in a hun-
gover haze in a bed awash in a stranger's blood and OD'd.

He did, not the character, although he'd already told me the man
would kill himself. There was no way out.

Pay attention, my brain yelled. *Wake up! He's telling you something
important.*

There'd been so many cries of wolf that I'd trained myself to
ignore them, to tamp down the rising panic and keep going. I became
a master of denial.

In the beginning, I had an itchy feeling that something wasn't
right. I walked around the house searching for something to explain
it—half a dozen missing spoons, drops of blood on the carpet in his
room. "Something is wrong," I said. My husband laughed at me.

Later, though, he would jump in the car at two in the morning and drive to Pittsburgh like a madman, trawling up and down
the hilly streets searching for his boy, expecting to find him lying

comatose in an alley. By the time we understood what was happening, it was too late.

Mark was fifteen when he told me I couldn't save him. Midway through his first rehab and already adept at the language of rationalization, he explained the tidal regularity of relapses I should expect. I never forgot what he said. "I'll never be recovered."

When he sent me a link to his novel, we exchanged texts, did some messing with his Google doc, and a little back and forth with him accepting and rejecting changes, holding onto his idiosyncratic grammar and plot leaps. He wasn't comfortable with edits, and I was cautious about making them.

Commenting, that weak substitute for action, seemed like it might work, and replying, the introvert's preferred method of communication, stood in for conversation. After all, we were only talking about a story.

We had one phone call about the story in early June. I was startled by how much his voice sounded like his brother's, by how much I wanted him to be okay, and for this project to be the bridge to safety.

"I've got two weeks to write it," he said.

"Who's chasing you?" I asked.

He said nothing, but I heard the footfalls of whatever it was in the dense silence that followed.

"No one can write a novel in two weeks," I said. "No matter what anyone tells you. A first novel can take years to crank out. Revisions take months. You've got stuff to say. Give yourself a year."

I thought it was enough encouragement that I took his writing seriously. I thought that purpose would give him time to work out whatever else was going on.

That's how we'd always gotten by, one year at a time, me reminding myself never to ask him for anything, never expect anything, never yield anything.

The last time we talked, he reminded me that I'd told his dad he was the real deal, how I took the first story he wrote to my bedroom and closed the door to read it alone, undisturbed by the customary hullabaloo in our household.

That was all he needed from me—the acknowledgment that he was more than his addiction. I saw him, the real him beneath the history and drama, the him he could be, the one for whom I held the space open. He had a way of coming back from beyond that lulled me into believing he'd make it. I told myself he'd step into himself one day. He'd make it to forty-five, that magic year we'd been told when sometimes people change.

Maybe the heroin was to celebrate something. Did it occur to him that it was laced with Fentanyl and could kill him? He was always going there; the slow suiciding of the way he lived guaranteed to yield this outcome sooner rather than later. It was just a question of where and who would be there when it happened.

My dead husband's cell phone rang at 3 A.M. the day after his funeral service. A woman said, "Your son was found on the street." Overdose, the nurse said. They got to him in time. He was in a medical coma to detox, but he would live.

I remembered all the other times—how he looked with a tube down his throat, how the nurse, social worker, and girlfriend had fluttered around him, how my husband's face went gray, and he sat with his hand over his eyes.

My stepson had never lacked attention. Women whose beauty, class, or education might have rendered him invisible to them flocked to him, thrumming to the palpable danger, his dark charm a match for their wild hearts. Later, they would tear themselves away to save their sanity.

Years ago, I'd stopped trying to console the women when they called me, sobbing that he'd stolen their money, cars, or TVs. Their self-esteem. How could I tell them they weren't who he was looking for and that the only way he could find her was to destroy them?

In his fiction, the girl was always getting on a bus, always leaving him running behind, hand extended, calling for her to wait. The real-life women who loved him couldn't compete with the perfume of her memory, even if he'd made her up, even if that scent was the only thing he had left of the mother who'd abandoned him.

In the end, heroin snuffed out his life. But he went like a man on a date with a woman he'd been longing for to a hotel where they could be alone for hours and hours. I imagine him telling everyone he was going to a party and picture him dressing up for it. He'd been chasing euphoria all his life, and he ran straight into her arms, all his synapses lighting up in anticipation. He almost made it to forty.

I don't know if he surrendered without a whimper. He was alone. The final image of him sprawled on the hotel bed belongs to the real woman he left behind, the one who sensed something was wrong and found him, who made that first call to the police, who screamed in her car on the way to his grave.

MAY THERE BE ABUNDANT PEACE

In my favorite crepe café, wooden tables are crammed together, and strangers sit shoulder to shoulder in every seat. Forks clink against white porcelain plates—casual chatter rackets from wall to wall. I order the spinach and artichoke crepe. My sister chooses crab. There's a crisp green salad on the side with a creamy lemon dressing.

We both have a glass of the chilled house white. Light from the front windows pings off the glasses as we lift them to our lips. The same light filters through her blonde hair. I'm always surprised by the clarity of her blue eyes and the delicate way she eats. And then I remember I'm the barbarian who doesn't quite fit.

Through the open café door comes the sound of ropes clanking against spars on sailboats docked at the Annapolis marina at the end of Duke Street, which opens to the sparkling blue Chesapeake Bay. Tourists stroll by the window, and I watch a man raise his arm in recognition and shout, "Ambrose, wait up!" His sneakered feet pound over the pavement. I take a sip of wine.

"Remember when . . . ," I say to Sarah, thinking of the time we ate breakfast at the Treaty of Paris restaurant up the street from here on the morning I went to court to divorce my first husband. The Federalist courtroom was empty except for us, two attorneys, and the judge. Legacy spider webs draped the upper balconies. Afterward, in the restaurant, thick steam rose from an opened popover and fogged the silver teapot on our table. That restaurant is gone now.

My sister waves her hand like a magic wand. "I don't remember my childhood. Nothing," she says, "not till I'm fifteen." She erases me. It's "her" childhood, not ours.

We were in our thirties, the decade when notions of perfection died. She's right. We've always had separate lives. Even when we shared

155

the same bedroom, we existed in two different realities. Sometimes I wonder where she was all those years I have no memories of her. Two years younger than me, Sarah and I have one thing in common: we grew up in the same climate, like dates and olives.

We meet once a year for lunch at this café, even if we have nothing new to say. We saw each other for Christmas, bar mitzvahs, weddings, Mother's Day until our mother died, and funerals. We no longer hug but lean in each other's direction as if the signifier of affection is the same as love.

That is until yesterday when she died at the ripe old age of eighty-five. We're separated now, not only by geography and temperament but by a state of being. Somehow her death makes her more accessible. I search for memories of her like an old woman who looks for the chicken she is sure she purchased for dinner and finds instead the deck of cards she put in the refrigerator. Sarah told me this joke. Despite all our differences, she could always make me laugh.

I look around me and judge the day by light filtering through curtains. I try to guess the hour. I'm usually wrong. It can be eight o'clock in the morning, nine-thirty, or even eleven. Light is unreliable. A dark winter day is still night for me, and I go back to sleep. Even the season is an open question.

This morning I lie on the bed, aware of my wakefulness. I would rather be dreaming. I set myself a series of questions. What is my name? Where do I live? Who is the president? What day is it? I don't know why I care. The answers don't matter. They won't change the world or the small universe of memory I shuttle through with the speed of teleportation. One moment I'm here, infirm, hobbled by age, and terrified of falling down the stairs. The next, I'm flying downhill on my bicycle, yodeling with glee, freedom like a kite bobbing above me.

I remind myself that my son is coming to take me to Sarah's funeral. At eighty-seven, I don't drive anymore. I fumble while making my cup of coffee. My hand trembles, and I spill half the coffee on the counter. Cleaning the mess is exhausting. I think about leaving it until later, but I don't. The idea of order still controls me, the comfort of it, the serenity it creates around me.

For most of my life, I fled the chaos, even the chaos I made, moving from house to house before cobwebs formed in ceiling corners. I've made my peace here in this house where I've lived for thirty years. I have a still life, deliberately arranged. I'm caught in my web, a kind of aging chrysalis. Will I grow wings after this?

I walk through my rooms, my back so bent that unless I lift my chin, making my head an apostrophe for the noun of my body, I'll see only the floor. I'm checking for ghosts, for the trail of fog they leave behind, for messages Sarah meant me to see.

Today, I've promised myself I'll start reading my aunt Mellie's novel. Something about Sarah's death brought me to this. I've had the box of six hundred typed pages in my hall closet for twenty years, unopened. Mellie gave it to my mother before she died. My mother gave it to me without reading it. I've been avoiding the effort, the obligation, and anticipated disappointment. I've waited so long; perhaps there's no longer any reason to read it. Still, it's an assignment I must complete before I die. There must be a reason my mother gave it to me. Nothing she did was innocent. My sister's death presses on me. Time presses on me. There are still open questions, even if I don't want the answers.

I remove the top of the tall, green box and pull out the manuscript in handfuls, stacking it on the dining room table. I need space for this. The manuscript is five inches high, its pages as thin as skin browned with age spots. The dust is dry in my mouth. Out of the window, in the greening park of my backyard, my trees are tall and wide, growing larger than anyone ever guessed they would. I want my oak trees to live a thousand years. The world, I'm convinced, will continue without me, glad to see my back.

My eyes fall on a sentence of the manuscript two paragraphs down that springs out of the text as if typed in red italics. "Mellie pushed her six-week-old infant into Zuzu's arms." My pulse is thready, erratic, and I slip into memory.

I'm sitting on a wooden sled, my arms wrapped tightly around Sarah. It's snowing. White snowflakes coat her snowsuit hood. I stick out my tongue to catch snowflakes as they fall. My cheeks are wet with them. They catch on my eyelashes and melt, making everything I see into stars.

My mother is pulling the sled and laughing. She runs faster. I grip the side of the sled with one hand and my sister with the other. I wrap my legs tighter around her. We're going downhill. My mother goes faster, her legs pumping, her laughter louder, wilder. She looks back at us over her shoulder. Her eyes are gleaming, her cheeks red. She seems happy, then more than happy. She grins too much. I feel something cold grab inside my chest and know that's fear. The sled turns over, and we topple onto the snow-covered ground. My mother laughs in ragged half sobs, unable to catch her breath.

The phone rings. My son's calling to remind me he's on his way, bringing me back to the present. He's such a good son. He even reminds me that I should wear outdoor clothes. We both know that means a dress and shoes instead of sweatpants, a sweater, and slippers. He's careful with me, his language a warm shawl around my shoulders.

I remember my stepmother sending me back upstairs to change for my father's funeral. She stared in disbelief at my jeans as I came down the stairs. "You can't wear that." I was thirty. She was still the authority. "Go back upstairs and put on something respectable." I complied. Sometimes I just needed someone to tell me the rules.

In the mirror on the dining room wall, I see I'm wearing a dress—what a relief. I go back to staring at the first page of my aunt's manuscript, but I'm not reading.

Instead, I'm climbing up onto the sofa with the Little Golden Book I want my mother to read to me. On the cover is a drawing of a mother and father, a boy, a girl, and a dog. They live in a cottage with a white picket fence around it. Trees line the street. On the inside pages, the father rakes leaves, and the son helps him. The mother does dishes, and the daughter dries them. A dog scampers around. Everyone smiles. I understand the book without the words, but I want to hear the words. There's a parade coming. Everyone's getting ready.

"I won't read this book to you," my mother says.

"Why?" I ask.

She hands the book back to me. "This is a book about a happy family," she says. "We're not a happy family."

I never forget this.

I re-read the sentence in my aunt's manuscript. Is this the answer to questions I've been asking all my life? I remind myself that it's a novel, and the writer wants to plunge the reader directly into the heat of the conflict. Still, I tremble. Truth is the heart of every novel. Is this the truth or simply the decorated box that holds it? I sip my coffee and stare at the mountains.

I'm transported instantly to a time when I was twelve. I was standing rigid, my head and shoulders leaning slightly forward from the waist toward my mother, my arms clenched at my sides. I'm screaming, "I must be adopted. I can't be your child. No mother would treat her child the way you treat me. . . ."

Of course, I'm wrong about that. I read yesterday about a woman who let her boyfriend throw her infant against the wall and then lock the child in a closet until he died. They wrapped the baby in a green trash bag and threw him in the dumpster behind the nearest fast food place.

I got off easy.

I survived.

My eyes track the words in my aunt's novel as if they're written in another language I must decode. The effort wearies me. I put the page down on the table—mountains in the distance beckon to me. I get up and walk out onto the back porch to inhale the peaceful view, thinking about my childhood.

A blonde with blue eyes and pale skin, my sister is the positive of my negative. She's the good child, the one who did what she was told, never talked back, or had to wash the floors, and never hung wash on the line when it was so cold her wet fingers froze to clothespins. Perhaps I deliberately excised her from my memory. I remember pouring a glass of milk over her head. There's a limit to the amount of perfection I can take.

We used to sit on our twin beds early on Saturday mornings and read until our mother summoned us. Our cotton pajamas are striped, our hair tangled messes. We consumed all the *Bobbsey Twins* books, *Bambi*, and all the *Nancy Drew* mysteries as if they were food and we were starving. We knew all these books word for word.

Leaping onto her bed, Sarah crouched, her arms raised in a menacing gesture, acting out one of the scenes in a *Nancy Drew* mystery. "You'll pay for this, Nancy Drew," she snarled, her face twisted to make the right sounds. "You'll see. One day I'm going to get you."

For a second, I'm convinced she's Nathan Gombit. We laugh, delighted with her perfect performance. From the kitchen, my mother calls out, "Are you laughing at me? I know what you're doing."

We laugh into our pillows until they're wet with tears.

I turn back to the manuscript but the words both snare and repel me. Something raises the hairs on the back of my neck and keeps me from taking in what's right in front of me. My mother didn't read this manuscript. She didn't want to know what her oldest sister had to say, even though she inherited all her money when she died.

How little I know about my sister. I recall her telling me at lunch shortly after my father's death fifty years ago, "I don't care about your life. Please don't tell me about it." She took a tiny bite of her salad and looked out the window as she chewed. "Anyway," she said, "nobody likes you."

My mind leaps to another memory.

My mother takes me on the bus to a tall brick house. We walk up steep brown steps, and a black door opens. A woman squats and unbuttons my coat. She tells me my favorite purple jumper is pretty and gives me a tablespoon of cod liver oil. My face revolts. She points to a water fountain.

She takes my hand and leads me to a room off the entrance. I sit at a long table with other children, a bowl of oatmeal in front of me. I watch the children, amazed by how they hold their spoons and put food in their mouths. I can't eat. I'm sure my mother is going to leave me here.

Our classroom is upstairs. I hold onto the metal vines beneath the banister to climb the stairs. The room is larger than any room I've ever seen, with a place to read, a place for toys, a place for cots. There's one huge bathroom, and all the boys and girls line up together to take turns sitting on the toilet. I'm too embarrassed to use it.

When we go outside to play, we go downstairs and through a room where Sarah stands in a crib in a room full of cribs. She's not crying. She holds onto the crib rail, staring at me. I want to grab her out of there and run away as fast as I can. I want to be the one who saves us.

I make toast and then forget about the toast until I hear the bread pop out of the toaster. My hand trembles, and the knife is heavy. I smear butter on the bread. The plate wobbles in my hand when I carry it to the table. I tell myself out loud, "Stop that." As if I ever had that kind of control.

In the blink of an eye, I'm a sophomore walking home from high school. I've made a place for myself with the nerds in class, but during lunch hour, I hang out with the bad kids—the ones who curse, snap their gum, wear makeup, and aren't going to college. I want to keep my options open.

My sister stands unmoving outside the house where our second-floor apartment is. Two-story houses and trees line Schley Street in Newark's Weequahic section. We're just ten blocks from both our schools. My Aunt Ellie, the beauty, who eats cantaloupe and London broil for dinner on a weeknight, lives in an apartment building near the high school. We can walk there. We're respectable.

Sarah, who goes to the middle school, walks away from our house, toward me, instead of going inside. I stop to say hello. Her face is almost the blue color of skim milk, paler than she usually is. I wonder if she's sick. She's thin and fragile—that's what my mother always says—and allergic to everything, even strawberries, my favorite fruit. I ask if she's going to the library.

She nods. "Mom's inside," she says, her eyes wide with the warning: *She's on a rampage.*

During those years, I frequently spent time with my friend, Ann, who has two parents and a brother and seems to know things about how to dress and walk and talk that I don't know. I watch her carefully, trying to learn how to be normal. Her family keeps kosher, and I'm forever putting my dish in the wrong place when I clear it. They're kind to me, though, the way you would be kind to a stray cat, and don't ask any questions when I show up at nine at night drenched from the pouring rain. My red shoes bleed on their kitchen floor. Ann's mother hands me a towel for my hair and calls my mother.

"You can stay here tonight," she tells me when she hangs up the phone. We both know my mother doesn't care where I am.

At the beginning of our first summer in the Schley Street apartment, my mother sends us away to overnight camp. Sarah and I are in separate bungalows and eat at different tables in the dining hall. The food is bland, and my stomach feels hollow all the time. When Sarah goes to the infirmary, I write my father a postcard telling him she's sick. I beg him to bring us home. "We can stay with you," I plead, "Mom will never know." He visits on parents' weekend instead and goes home without us.

The following summer, we come home from camp to a completely different house, one block from the high school Sarah and I now both attend. It's a fancier street, all single-family homes with driveways, more appropriate to my mother's new status. She has married husband number four.

Down the block, there's a boy in my class whose father has a pool table and a den decorated with the stuffed heads of animals he killed on an African safari. My classmate feeds me snacks of elegant canapés and sparkling mineral water and reads aloud to me from *Finnegan's Wake.* I worry I'm another trophy for his walls. He's confused; it's my sister he wants to date.

My son touches my shoulder. I didn't hear him come into the house. "Time to go, Mom," he says. He helps me out of the chair and into my coat. His wife and my grandson embrace me, and for a minute, I have found the meaning to everything, the whole point, the reason for being. I've been searching for this memory, where my son places my brand new grandson in my arms, and all the sorrow I've ever felt is overwhelmed by joy.

My sister's plain wooden casket is closed. The pocket on my nephew's shirt is torn. His eyes are red-rimmed—such a sweet boy. We go to the cemetery, and my sons guide me to my seat under the canopy. I weep, as always, when I hear the *Kaddish*, but my lips are numb, and I don't have breath enough for speech. The casket is lowered into the ground, and my sons throw dirt over the coffin for me.

My sister squats on the beach, her knees tucked under her chin. The slightest ripples from waves lap her toes. She looks up at me. Her blue eyes reflect the sky and sea. A gull rides the air above us. My mouth is full of sweetness.

WHAT SHE COULDN'T KNOW

A white rectangular box arrives by UPS, wrapped round and round in translucent tape. It's the kind of box that might contain the top of a wedding cake, frozen for a year, to be opened on the first anniversary. Or maybe it holds lost slippers, a riding hat, or perishable fruit. It could be anything. Perhaps it's a gift of unbearable love from the universe. I imagine light leaking from it. It's not heavy. I lift it off the front porch step where the delivery man left it and carry it into the house.

My dead sister is listed as the sender. My pulse quickens. I slice at the tape, the box cutter shaking in my hand. *Cut away from your body,* I hear my husband saying. And when it's clear that at eighty-seven, I don't have sufficient dexterity to do that, I grip the box against me with one hand and slice toward my belly, thinking, *What the hell? What's the worst that will happen? I'll die.* In my head, I hear my mother cackle.

Inside the box, several layers of bubble wrap enshroud a long manila envelope like an unearthed mummy prepared for transportation to a museum. I unwind it slowly, thinking *my sister was never this careful with anything.* The handwriting on the slim envelope is not hers. It's young and bold and takes up space as if space is its birthright, unlike the cramped, slanted scrawl my sister and I share—the handwriting of children who cowered in corners hoping to be ignored.

All the women in my family have the same handwriting. Letters from my aunts and mother display the same slant, the same descendent legs of p and g, the loopless l—marks as identifiable as a genetic signature, the fingerprint of our tribe's history. My sons' handwriting is like their father's: anarchic, letters freely detaching themselves from the root of symbolic meaning.

165

"Mom wanted you to have this," is printed on the envelope. It's signed simply, "Bill."

I sit in my green kitchen chair, trying to remember who Bill is. It requires all my strength, taking me back through corridors of memories that call to me like ghosts. It's work to stay on course. I smile when I find the memory.

I'm rushing up the cement stairs to my sister's third-floor apartment, my arms full of flowers and gifts. I miss a step, slamming my shin against the stair's metal tip, but I don't stop until I arrive at her door.

Knocking, I turn the knob and see Sarah with an infant in her arms, a look of beatitude and peace on her face. This child was all she ever wanted, and now she had it. *Transformed by love,* I thought and opened my arms for the baby.

Bill, I recall now, is my nephew, my sister's son. He's the one who sent what she left for me.

I rip open the envelope and pull out ten typed onion-skin pages, numbered at the top, the first chapter of an old manuscript that looks familiar, but I can't immediately place it. The pages shake in my hand. My sister's handwriting slants across the bright pink paper stuck on the first page:

I decided you should have this. I found it in Mom's things after she died. I might be sorry I kept it from you, but then again, I might not be. According to Mom, Aunt Mellie wrote it, but it reads more like Uncle Willie did. Mom is probably the character called Zuzu. Perhaps the story's true. If so, it would change everything. You decide for yourself if it still matters to you.

Sarah had been the executor of our mother's will. That was sixteen years ago. I never asked what she did with Mom's things. When my sister died, Bill was left to sort out her stuff. I stop breathing for a second, realizing she'd kept this document from me all this time. The story was a secret she hoarded, a bomb to be delivered third hand and set to detonate when she was safely away. But she might be right about one thing; it might not matter to me at this point.

I put the envelope and pages on the kitchen table and fix myself a cup of coffee. I add cream and sugar and feel flutters in my stomach—the spoon clinks against the side of my mug in time with the tremors of my hand.

I will read it, I tell myself as I stare out the window at the unmoving mountains. *I can do it, safe here, years from my childhood and far away.* Puttering around my aging house situated in the perfect tree-lined neighborhood, nestled on a hill between two rivers, a place I could never have imagined being, my days are filled with reading, writing, daydreaming, and watering my plants. I've achieved a modicum of peace. Taking three sips of coffee, I gaze out the window and find an unexpected memory.

I hold up my hand and tick off for my stepmother the reasons I have to leave her house this minute. "If I don't leave right now, I'll be late for my son's college graduation." I pause to watch her face.

Nothing. She's not buying it.

"Yesterday's 250-mile drive with Jake and Sarah in the car is nothing compared to dodging cars going ninety-five miles an hour on the Turnpike through New Jersey to the tunnel exit."

"I'll drive," she offers.

I shake my head. *That's worse*, I think, remembering when she refused to make a left onto the main road because the sign warned her to stay to the right of the center island, but I bite my tongue, having learned by now that truth doesn't work with her. I continue my list. In my family, one must always have reasons.

"There's the hour-long wait to get through the toll. Sitting at a dead stop inside the Holland tunnel gives me the creeps. The river might seep through the tiles, flooding the tunnel, leaving us no way out."

My stepmother rolls her eyes. I know what she's thinking: I'm such a drama queen.

"Frenetic cross-town traffic to the bridge makes me sweat." I'm up to my fifth finger. "I never know which way to turn. I always get lost in Brooklyn."

She shakes her head. I fill her with sorrow.

"I need to leave enough time to overcome small disasters, like flat tires and blown gaskets, enough time to stop and ask a kid on a bike for directions."

She looks down at the floor, saddened that I still talk to strangers.

"And Sarah isn't ready to go because she never is. She'll make me late." That's how she controls everything, just like my mother, forcing me to wait for her, tapping my toes, pacing the room, dreading her entrance.

I don't tell my stepmother the real reason: This day needs to be about my son, not them, not me. I need to be on time for him, and I don't have time to argue.

My stepmother gives me her usual *Oh, my God, who is this kid?* look she's been using for thirty-five years, ever since she married my father. "Don't worry," she says, trying to calm me. "We've got plenty of time. We'll have breakfast. I'll go into town for bagels. You want a salt, right?"

I don't want to eat breakfast with my stepmother. I want to be with my son. Anyway, I never believe her about anything. I wait as long as I can bear and then leave two tickets for the graduation ceremony on the kitchen table with a note: *We'll see you there.*

The drive only takes an hour; the tunnel doesn't leak. My anxiety lifts when I spot my son hanging half out of his third-floor apartment window, waving both arms to get my attention. "Park here," he yells and points. He's been watching out for me—the bright flag of his exuberance flaps in the air.

I made it in time. We're safe. I didn't screw this up or embarrass him.

We walk together to the college grounds, my pride blinking like a neon sign. Every cheer in the world springs into my mouth when my son crosses the stage. *G-o-o-o-a-a-a-l!* I yell in my head, but I want to shout it at the top of my voice. "Hooray! Hallelujah!" I stand and whistle and clap. My sons, the graduate on stage and the younger one next to me, grin. They grew up with me. I can't embarrass them. My sister and stepmother, who arrived in time to use the seats I saved for them, turn their faces away, pretending they're not with me.

After the ceremony, Sarah says they're leaving. Immediately. They have other more important things to do. My sons' faces mirror my surprise.

"You're not going to celebrate with us?" I ask, incredulous that they would skip the party to spite me.

The corners of my sister's mouth turn down. My stepmother shakes her head and gives me her *"You're such a disappointment"* look. A world of perpetually dashed expectations orbits between us. I'm tangled in the thought that I'm supposed to please her, but I remember how she always held herself aloof as if she were better than me and her daughters had a right to a future to which I could never aspire. My children watch me. What I do affects them in ways I can't predict. I want them to be normal, free, and unencumbered by my past mistakes. I inhale, close my eyes, and leap.

Linking arms with my sons, I tell my sister, "Then we'll celebrate on our own."

We turn to go, and my new graduate says, "Whew. I thought for a minute you were going to mark off twenty paces." Our laughter flies out behind us as we walk away.

By the time I get back to my stepmother's house, they've eaten dinner and are speaking to me in single syllables. The next day, Sarah fumes in my car's back seat, unwilling to breathe the same air I do. Her unspeakable fury rubs against my neck for the five-hour drive.

Weeks later, in the middle of doing something else, I remember how she stood with me in court for my divorce hearing, how afterward, we celebrated in a tablecloth restaurant with real silverware and flowers on the table. We drank Mimosas and ate steaming hot popovers spread with whipped butter and orange marmalade.

I call her. "This is silly. I don't even know why you're mad at me."

"You laughed at me," she says. "You left me there alone, and you laughed at me." She pauses, looking for more reasons. "You encouraged your sons to disrespect me."

My face freezes. I'm stunned by her words. In my head, I hear my father say, *Tell your sister you're sorry.* The sentence sticks in my throat—clogged by objections that she started it, that I didn't do anything wrong—and then burns in my chest when I comply.

"What do I need to do to resolve this?" I ask.

"I want you to get down on your knees and beg for my forgiveness."

As if she were my master or God and I had no intrinsic right to be in the world without her blessing. Relieved at my clarity, I say, "I'm not going to do that," and hang up the phone.

"I might be sorry . . . but, then again, I might not be," taunts my sister's note on the manuscript. Even if she wasn't interested in my life, I invited her into it over and over. I see her standing at the stove in my kitchen making potato *latkes* for Chanukah, slapping the cakes between her hands, dropping them in the sizzling oil, and singing the *latke* song.

What would it have cost me to say I'm sorry? What would we have gained? We tried, I tell myself. Sometimes, we tried; sometimes, we failed. I forgive her in advance without knowing what lurks on the pages she sent me. I take another sip of coffee and read the story she withheld for over a decade.

White smoke from the train's black engine plumed over the cars as it hissed into the station, enveloping two women standing on the platform and then lifting, little by little, revealing them as if they'd just emerged from a cloud.

Zuzu, wearing a yellow, gossamer dress that swirled at her knees, jiggled her body, eager to be gone. Even her fingertips wiggled. She couldn't bear to be in one place too long. Bright California sunlight kissed her bare arms.

Mellie pushed her six-week-old infant into those arms.

Zuzu startled, eyebrows knit together in annoyance and perplexity. "What are you doing?"

Mellie, anxious, was intent on executing her plan and leaving. "I can't keep her," she said. "I have a career. Jim doesn't want any children." Dark circles under her eyes accentuated a long nose on a paler than normal face and exposed her exhaustion.

To a stranger's eye, the women looked unrelated, certainly not sisters; the younger woman was taller, broader, and more conscious of the space she occupied.

Zuzu's brown eyes widened. "Mellie, that's not my problem." But she rocked the baby without thinking, singing under her breath, her shoulders and hips moving to the rhythm of the popular tune she hummed. Searching the crowd, Zuzu tossed her head, and her shining auburn curls danced in the air.

Mellie, constantly assessing, watched her. Thirteen years her junior, Zuzu was bored by responsibility and waiting. She liked sparkly things, loud music, and dancing with handsome men, many men. The more, the merrier. She craved attention, and men's adoration suited her. The war was over, the air was alive with jubilation, and she was raring to go. Her eyes shone every time a man looked at her. Her lips parted. She was an open invitation.

Mellie took two steps away from Zuzu and tugged on her jacket hem with both hands as if, her arms now empty, she could reclaim herself by straightening it. Dressed in her customary navy-blue suit over a carefully ironed white blouse buttoned to the top, she pressed her lips together; her eyes narrowed with intent. "Please take her."

"What? You mean take her away with me? Are you kidding?"

For two weeks, Mellie had planned to give the child to Zuzu, but it was harder to do than she expected. If she were honest with herself, she'd planned to give the child away the moment she'd realized she was pregnant. Zuzu taking the child was the logical solution.

She had considered leaving the baby with the Sisters of Mercy, whose L.A. orphanage was still taking children, but she couldn't do it. It wasn't that she had difficulty with the idea of abandoning her child. The problem was that they might have turned her away. She was married and had a home and a good income. The nuns would tell her it was a sin to orphan the child when there were living parents who could afford to keep her. Their disapproval wouldn't be good for her reputation. There were no other options. Mellie couldn't see herself leaving the child in a basket by the orphanage door. That was so trite. Besides, someone might see her.

She had to convince Zuzu to take the baby. "I can't keep her."

The baby smiled in her sleep.

"She looks like Jim," Zuzu said. She looked up at her sister. "He's cuter than you. Really, Mellie, I don't know what he sees in you."

"Please, Zuzu." Mellie put her hand on her sister's arm. "See how she likes you."

Zuzu's lips curled down at the corners, and she looked around the platform for the man she hoped would come to see her off, the man who courted her during her visit to Los Angeles when she was supposed to be helping Mellie with the new baby. He took her for drives along the beach road in his Cadillac convertible and turned her head. They had sex in the back seat of his car at the overlook on Mulholland Drive. Zuzu believed in Hollywood endings. She was sure this man was her prince, and he would arrive at the pumpkin hour to save her from a life of drudgery, like clerking behind the ladies' lingerie counter in a department store.

"Why didn't you talk to me about this before now? You had two whole months." She held the baby out to Mellie, who stepped back and shook her head, her empty hands locked behind her to make sure she wouldn't reach out for her baby.

The child, wrapped in a cocoon of pink flannel, flung one arm in the air, and her eyelids fluttered. Zuzu was right. She looked like Jim, a beautiful baby with cream-colored skin, blonde hair, huge dark eyes, and long lashes. Mellie could almost have loved her if she had been someone else's child, like a friend's dog she might happily pet when she visited.

But she couldn't keep her. The baby interfered with her marriage. Throughout her pregnancy, her husband railed at her that she should have been more careful, should have taken precautions. It takes two to tango, she thought but held her tongue.

What she wanted to do wasn't unheard of in Europe or among the actresses she represented. She wanted her sister to bring up the baby as her own. She never admitted it to any of her friends, but her handsome second husband, six years younger than her, would never have married or touched her if she weren't a rich woman, free of all encumbrances. She thanked her dead first husband every day for his industry.

Zuzu glanced around one more time, hoping to spot her prince charming striding toward her across the platform. She looked up at the cloudless blue sky and shaded her eyes with one hand. California-struck by palm trees, the light off of the ocean, bare bodies, and day after day of sun, she missed the place even before she left it. She sighed and hugged the baby.

Mellie understood what her sister was feeling. She came to L.A. from cold, dirty New Jersey with her first husband. The moment they disembarked from the train, shucking off her coat, she was liberated. Not to have her legs freeze waiting for a bus to take her downtown in winter, not to scurry along the sidewalk like litter in the wind was bliss. But it wasn't the mild weather, abundant flowers, or bright sunlight that turned her head.

The lie seduced her, although endless days of sunshine made it much easier to pretend. Everyone pretended. In California, she could leave the past behind and be whomever she wanted. She didn't have to be a Jewess born in Europe whose parents immigrated to America and lost the little they had in the Depression. She could be a rich lawyer whose husband played polo. She could be Catholic and hang out with movie stars at their villas on the Palisades overlooking the Pacific. She could play bridge and write plays. Three thousand miles would keep her embarrassing, dysfunctional family at bay.

The train whistle blared. The conductor blew his tinny whistle and cried, "All aboard!"

"Look, I'll pay you," Mellie said, thinking of how her husband groaned when the baby cried in the night, how he turned his back on her.

Zuzu's eyes widened. She'd always been good with numbers. "You'll pay me to take your child? How much?"

"More than you have now, which is nothing, with no prospects of ever earning very much. Enough that you won't have to work if you're careful." Mellie took a breath. Her mouth was dry. She licked her lips and sweetened the deal. "I'll pay you four hundred dollars a month. You can live comfortably on that. It'll cover your rent, food, clothes, whatever. Keep the child until she's eighteen. Then she's on her own."

Mellie, small and plain, was an observer of the world. Zuzu was beautiful in a wild, untamed way. Danger and heat radiated from her. Men's eyes followed her anywhere she went. Mellie watched her sister look back at men over her shoulder as she sashayed away from them. Zuzu was going home empty-handed unless she took the baby. Mellie knew this was a gamble, but none of Zuzu's other schemes had panned out. Certainly not dropping out of school, marrying a jazz musician at seventeen, and divorcing him two years later.

Zuzu closed her eyes and tilted her head, considering the arrangement, silently estimating how much the deal was worth to her. The baby sighed and turned her head.

Mellie sweetened her offer. "I'll keep paying you even if you get married."

Zuzu calculated how many pretty dresses and sparkling necklaces the money would buy. She could see herself with rhinestone earrings dangling along her neck. Mellie didn't say the money was to support the child.

The train boarded with the usual tumult of hissing brakes, goodbyes, and calls from the conductor. People rushed past them carrying luggage.

Zuzu looked around at everyone moving as a herd, then at Mellie, and shrugged. She looked down at Mellie's daughter in her arms. "How hard can it be? What have I got to lose?"

Mellie thought of her answers—her freedom, her patience, her sense of self—all the things she didn't want to lose, but she didn't say anything. She put the diaper bag strap on Zuzu's shoulder and walked her toward the train.

"There's formula you'll have to mix with water and enough diapers for a week and clothes and blankets. You're supposed to keep her swaddled. Make sure you feed her every four hours and change her diaper. You know, like we practiced. Watch her head. And don't just walk away and forget her somewhere."

Zuzu shrugged off the instructions.

Mellie's chest cramped; she found it hard to speak. She may have been giving away her child, but she didn't want the baby to die. She shook off her sense of foreboding. *I'm freeing myself. It'll be okay. Zuzu won't harm the baby. Mama will step in.*

"Mellie, what do I tell people when I suddenly show up with a baby?"

"Tell them you fell in love with a lieutenant and married him before he shipped out to the Pacific. You've got photos of yourself with handsome men in uniform. Pick one. He died in a battle. Tell them his baby was born while you were out here, right when the Allied Forces defeated Hitler. People will love the story."

Zuzu already knew the story. It was the plot of all the newest movies. She smiled and nodded as if she understood the value of this version of things, what it would get her in sympathy and attention. She would portray a war widow and bask in the anticipated attention. Then she frowned. "What if I get tired of it? Will you take her back?"

The conductor waved for her to board. When he saw the baby in Zuzu's arms, he walked toward her to help, his broad face shiny with goodwill. Zuzu's eyes lit up. She tilted her head and looked at him helplessly. Mellie saw the whole picture of how her sister would do this.

She put a hand on Zuzu's arm to get her attention. "There are papers in the sack for you to sign," she said. "You sign them, and you get money for eighteen years. Have Willie and Mama witness your signature. Send the papers back to me after you sign them. Understand?"

Zuzu nodded, indignant. "Of course, I understand. It's a legal arrangement. Just because I didn't finish high school doesn't mean I'm an idiot." She went with the conductor, the baby light in her arms with his hand under her elbow, then paused on the train steps holding the baby. The baby waved one tiny arm in the air. From a distance, she already looked like the brave young war widow and mother.

"There's cash in the diaper bag in the same envelope as the agreement," Mellie said. "Call me when you get to Mama's. I told Willie you're coming with the baby." Mellie leaned forward to whisper in Zuzu's ear, "Never tell anyone this is my child. Never. No one. Not even her."

It took nearly a week and two transfers, lugging the baby and her suitcase from one track to another, to get from L.A. to Newark, New Jersey. Mellie didn't pay for a sleeper car, although she could easily have afforded it. Zuzu would have gone out of her mind if it weren't for returning GIs. Soldiers took turns holding the baby, changing her diapers, and feeding her from the bottle. Something about the tiny creature sleeping on a uniformed man's shoulder made Zuzu weepy. The story about her dead hero husband went over beautifully. The more she told it, the truer it seemed. She practiced by telling it to the baby.

"You're too cute to be a mother," a GI said, winking at her.

She grinned and rocked her shoulders. He stared at her breasts and put his hand flat on her back as if to claim her. She wrote her mother's phone number on his arm in eyebrow pencil, but he got off in Chicago and never called.

Soldiers let her sleep with her head on their shoulders; they helped her walk to the dining car with the baby. All those handsome, strong boys in their uniforms kissed her goodbye, one after the other, and she got off the train in Newark with the child, already wishing she'd told Mellie no. She planned to return the baby when her sister visited the east coast.

Willie, a year out of the Army and wearing a suit, was on the platform to meet her. He raised his hat when he saw her on the train step, wrapped his arm around her, clucked to the baby, and got a Red Cap to take the bags. They took a cab instead of the bus to their mother's apartment. Zuzu felt like a celebrity.

Her mother cried, cradled the baby, and talked Hungarian, German, and Yiddish to her. She kissed the baby's cheeks and smiled. Her face glowed.

Zuzu pulled the baby away from her mother and rocked her to show she knew what to do. She tossed her head. "I'm the one getting the money for her, Mama, so let's be clear about that."

Her mother's eyes widened, and she took a step back as if Zuzu had slapped her.

Willie looked up from his cup of coffee. "Nobody's saying anything different," he said in that calm voice nurses used to soothe the nerves of shell-shocked soldiers, the voice he learned during his recuperation in the VA hospital.

Zuzu looked at her mother over her shoulder. "Anyway, Mellie's probably already supporting you, Mama, right? You don't need to take my money."

Her mother wordlessly held her arms out for the baby. Zuzu, feeling everything was settled, handed the child back. A bassinet was set up in the corner of the living room, a hand-crocheted blanket folded over the side. With a start, Zuzu realized everyone knew about this arrangement in advance but her. Mellie had conned her, inviting her out to California on a pretext, knowing all the while what she had in mind.

Resolving to hate her sister forever, Zuzu took a bath and came out of her room in an off-the-shoulder, polka-dot dress purchased in California. Her shoulders still glowed from the sun. She twirled to show them how the dress flared around her legs. Willie's eyebrows arched up over widened blue eyes.

Her mother, sitting in her chair in the living room under the painting Willie had made, said, "Zuzu, *wass machst du*? What are you doing? Are you not tired?"

"I'm going to the Roseland Ballroom to dance," Zuzu said and twirled again so her mother and brother could see how full of life she was, ready for anything. "I have to see Broadway. I've been away so long."

Her mother's lips made a flat line between her cheeks; her face didn't glow for Zuzu the way it did for the baby. It never had, as far as Zuzu was concerned.

Willie's billboard face announced she wasn't supposed to go anywhere now. She had to take care of a baby. "It's a pretty rough crowd there these days," he said.

Zuzu wasn't going to listen to them. She'd let Mellie saddle her with the child, but that was enough. She needed free time. She needed to be somewhere else, away from them *and* the baby. They could take their turns. She'd been handling the baby for a week, a baby who wasn't even hers after all. She was doing Mellie a favor.

"Just leave me alone." She shrugged off their disapproval, picked up her small, gold-sequined purse, opened it to check that her lipstick and money were inside, and walked out of the apartment.

The dancehall was crowded and smelled like cigarettes, flowery perfume, and sweat. Globes of lights hanging from the ceiling swirled above them, and colors flashed across the walls and people's faces, making them seem like figments of her imagination. The band was loud, and the music wrapped her up and took her away. Within minutes, her dance card was full, and she whirled around the floor. Men made her laugh, fawned over her, bought her drinks, and found ways to touch her buttocks and breasts while they were dancing. She giggled and didn't object, craving the attention.

Zuzu got back to her mother's apartment at two in the morning, driven like a lady in the car of the last guy who danced with her. The white dots on her dress glowed in the moonlight. She gave him her mother's phone number and invited him to call her.

He leaned across the seat to kiss her. "See you soon, hot stuff."

When she looked back from the sidewalk, he was still watching her as he wiped lipstick off his lips with a folded white handkerchief. She twitched her hips for him, and he winked.

Inside the apartment, the baby squalled, and her mother walked up and down the small living room, rocking the child and humming a Strauss waltz. Zuzu heated a bottle, tested the temperature of the milk against the skin on her wrist, handed the bottle to her mother, and went to bed with rolled-up tissues stuffed in her ears and the pillow over her head.

Over the phone, Willie warned Mellie, "This will never work. Zuzu's not . . . she's *not* mother material. She can't do this." He was thousands of miles away from his oldest sister but not far enough to allay his fury. Mellie had done an incomprehensible thing. He knew she wouldn't back down, that she had made him complicit, and he would never forgive her.

"It's been a week," Mellie said. "Give it time."

"She never picks the baby up. She lets her cry for hours. Mama's too old to take care of an infant, but she's trying. They're fighting. Mama weeps on the phone to me every day. You know how it is around Zuzu. She makes everyone crazy."

"I'm not taking the baby back," Mellie said, irritated that her smart brother couldn't figure this out. "Has she signed the guardian-ship agreement? Once Zuzu signs it, the child is hers. She gets the money, and I get my freedom."

"What about the baby?" Willie prodded. "What does she get?"

Mellie looked out of her bedroom window at another beautiful day. She was going to play tennis at the club, have lunch in an out-door café in the mountains, and watch her handsome husband race around on a horse in a polo match. She had already picked out the lemon-yellow linen dress she would wear and the matching hat and shoes. She didn't care about the baby.

She shook off the thought. It made her look bad. "Look, Willie, it's not like the baby is with a stranger. You're clever. Find a solution. Get Zuzu married off to someone older, more mature. She'll settle down. It'll be okay."

Willie hung up on his sister. He closed his eyes in exhaustion and saw an image of the man he would introduce to Zuzu. He was a good man, a Marine just out of the service, and handsome. Mellie was right. It might work. For the child's sake, it had to.

I put the last page of the story on my lap and sit with my eyes closed for a while. The world around me rocks. I find it hard to catch my breath.

When I come back to myself, my hand is on my chest as if it's holding in my heart. Hands trembling, I tear open the envelope to see if I missed any pages. There are five more pieces of paper, including a guardianship agreement my aunt and mother signed. The child's name is different from mine and different from the name on my birth certificate. The birth date is the same.

Did my mother, who is suddenly not my mother, change my name? Was there another child who died? It could all be fiction. I'll never know the truth. Anyone who knew is dead and would have been sworn to secrecy. Was this the story Willie was never supposed to tell me, the story I shouldn't believe?

I can't deal with this. I stand up without thinking, and yellowed pages flutter to the floor like peeled skin. I don't bother to pick them up. Not today, anyway. I walk away from the table onto the back porch and sit in the sun. It's the beginning of spring. A cool breeze soothes my cheeks. I can't get the story out of my mind.

What if my mother is not my mother? That means my sister is not my sister. My father, I already knew, is not my father. I belong to no one. No wonder I wasn't like them. Were they the gypsies who stole me? The ground shifts again.

I remember screaming at my mother, "I must be adopted. A real mother wouldn't treat me like this." The shock on her face. My whole life is a lie. A wave of yearning for what I never had engulfs me. To have a real family who loved me, to be the child in the Golden Book my mother wouldn't read to me. Who would I be if I were not me?

I sit very still, my hands in my lap, and pretend I'm dreaming. This never happened. I breathe in and out, searching for the calm I woke with, for the tranquility that has enveloped my recent days. But the voice in my head says, *I'm not who I think I am.* Later, I'll wake up from this strange dream, and I'll still be Irene, Zuzu's daughter, Mellie's niece, and my sister will be my sister by a different father. This is all just a twist on the story I know, the one embedded in my genes.

In the next second, my perspective flips and I see Mellie standing in the station, her arms empty, tears streaming down her face. I imagine her wiping her face with a clean, white handkerchief and walking briskly from the train station to her car, straightening her shoulders, thinking of what she's going to tell Jimmie. The shock on his face.

I walk through the house to gather my wits. Photographs of my children and grandchildren greet me everywhere. Arrayed around me is the family I made, the one to which I belong without question, the people I chose and birthed. My clan, blood of my blood. They comfort me. In a collage of photos, my mother hugs my young sons. There's no resemblance between them. But with the seismic force of all sudden discoveries, I know I'm as much her daughter as I am the daughter of my father, who wasn't my father, and Sarah is my sister by the rite of passage, by declaration, by memory. They are mine if I choose them.

My turmoil eases. The mountains are still there—their quiet solidity comforts me. Sometime in the afternoon, my son calls. All my love leaps into my chest the way it did the day he graduated. I hope the sound of my voice will carry it to him. I say hello, close my eyes, and listen to him. I don't need a story or reasons to understand our connection. This is what's true.

THE END

ACKNOWLEDGMENTS

Nine of the stories in this book were originally published in literary journals. My deep thanks to those editors for their encouragement and support.

"Learning by Heart" first published in *Fluent Magazine*, Vol 1, No. 2, Oct. 2012

"Unmentionables" first published by *The Delmarva Review*, Vol. 10, Nov. 2017

"Finding the Square Root of Everything" first published by *Temenos*, Fall 2017/Spring 2018

"Secondhand Gifts" first published in *Heartwood Literary Magazine,* Issue 6, Fall 2018

"May There Be Abundant Peace" first published by *The Delmarva Review*, Vol. 11, Nov. 2018

"The Physics of Things" first published in the 2019 *Anthology of Appalachian Writers*

"Looking for Bargains in the Cosmic Five and Dime" first published by *Women Arts Quarterly Journal,* Summer 2019

"Aurora Borealis" first published in *Masque & Spectacle*, Sept. 2019

"Going to the Dogs," first published in the 2022 *Anthology of Appalachian Writers*

Many thanks also to the readers and editors who selected this novel, under the title STRONGER IN HEAVEN, for the 2019 SFWP award shortlist and as a finalist for the 2020 Bakwin award.

I salute the genius of my writer friends K.P. Robbins, Catherine Baldau, Tara Bell, Frank Joseph, Linda Morefield, Solveig Eggerz, Katharine Lorr, Catherine Flanagan, Leslie Rollins, Bob Gibson, Phil Harvey, Stan Whatley, Deb Barger, and Lauren Woods for their hours of attention and invaluable feedback. They are the village in which my book babies grow up. A heartfelt bow to my sister, Carolyn Bross, for years of encouragement, to my editor, Abigail Henson, whose sharp eye and attention helped to shape the novel, and all those at Sunbury who made this project a reality.

My deepest gratitude always goes to my children without whom there'd be no point in writing about the astonishing beauty of an ordinary life.

ABOUT THE AUTHOR

GINNY FITE, besotted grandmother, Ravenclaw, and Divergent, is the author of seven novels, three collections of poetry, and a book of humorous essays on aging. She lives in Harpers Ferry, West Virginia.

Made in the USA
Columbia, SC
15 May 2023

16782657R00117